HER TEMPORARY HERO

OTHER BOOKS BY JENNIFER APODACA

THE BABY BARGAIN

HER TEMPORARY HERO

JENNIFER APODACA

Entangled Publishing, LLC
2614 South Timberline Road
Suite 109
Fort Collins, CO 80525
Visit our website at www.entangledpublishing.com.

Indulgence is an imprint of Entangled Publishing, LLC.

Edited by Alethea Spiridon Hopson and Kate Fall
Cover design by Heidi Stryker

ISBN 978-1501000218

Manufactured in the United States of America

First Edition July 2014

Chapter One

"Diapers are expensive, baby girl. What do you think about giving them up?"

Becky Holmes smiled at her daughter perched carefully on her hip, while dropping the precious diapers in the backseat of her weathered Toyota Corolla. Three months of experience had taught her to handle almost any task one-handed. Sophie babbled her answer while Becky secured her in the car seat. The baby's intense hazel eyes flecked with gray were full of mischief.

"Is that a no?" Fixing the shimmering lilac bow on her oh-so-kissable bald head, she laughed. "Then we'd better get home so I can work on that pageant dress, now hadn't we?" Setting a cloth book on Sophie's tummy, she backed out and closed the door. Once they got home, if the baby slept two hours, then she'd be able to finish the dress. With luck, she could deliver it tonight on her way to her cleaning job and—

Her back hit a warm object. Not a car. A man.

Elemental fear shot down her spine. Becky forced herself to breathe and angled her head enough to catch the reflection in the window of her car. Oh God. Fisting her car keys, she spun around and faced the man who'd put her in the hospital a year ago.

"Dylan, you're out." *Of prison.* This couldn't be happening. He'd taken a plea deal for a hit-and-run accident and been sentenced to a few years in prison. It'd only been five months since he went away. But there he stood, five feet, ten inches of boyish charm, unchecked arrogance, and a carefully cloaked snake-mean streak.

Becky wasn't afraid of snakes.

She was terrified of Dylan.

His sky blue eyes flicked past her to the backseat. "You're such a cliché, a dirt dumb ex-beauty queen. Of course I'm out. I'm a Ridgemont. By this time next year, that conviction will be overturned, and the state of Texas will be paying me for their grave error."

Culture and education flowed through his voice. But he wasn't totally wrong—she had been dirt dumb to believe that son and heir of the Ridgemont Empire had fallen in love with the scholarship girl from the trailer park. Even dumber not to see the signs of his vicious side. But she'd wised up and wasn't letting him hurt her baby.

Their baby.

"Okay." She needed to keep him calm and get away. *What did he want?* Becky looked around the grocery store parking lot, but there was no one to help. "I don't want to keep you if you're heading into the store. I need to get going."

Dylan curved the left half of his mouth. "Back to your

trailer with the new FOR SALE sign that your ugly ass dog likes to pee on? Or are you taking my kid to work with you tonight cleaning the Wyatt Medical group offices? You don't go to work until much later, so maybe you're going to your mom's new digs at the cemetery?"

Chills skittered down her spine. Greasy sickness coated her mouth. He knew where she lived, worked, and that her mom had died. "You've been following me." The words spilled out and her fear ratcheted up. And up. Until it pounded in her head with the beat of, *run, run, run.*

Dylan leaned in, slapping his hand on the roof of her car, lowering his voice to a whisper. "I have people to do whatever I need done. I know exactly where you are at all times in case I want to finish what we started the day you ratted me out to the cops over a useless bum that no one gave two shits about."

"You'll go back to prison if you touch me." Becky leaned against the door to keep baby Sophie safe from her father. That whole terrible night replayed in her brain...but the worst of it had been his cold callousness after he hit the man with his truck. Dylan had left him on the street in a pool of blood, driving away with Becky screaming in the passenger seat.

No, don't think about that, stay focused.

"Keep telling yourself that." He leaned so close she smelled coffee on his breath. "Oh, and you'd better start saying your good-byes to the brat. I have a team of lawyers working on getting full custody of the kid. You caused me major problems with my family by having it."

What? No! "You won't win." She wrapped her arms around her stomach, desperation hammering up her spine.

The thought of Sophie in his care was too much. Too awful. Losing Sophie would kill her, but her real fear was for her child's safety.

"You tried to destroy my life by ratting me out and having that kid after I told you to get rid of it. Payback's a bitch." He turned and strode off.

Becky ran around her car, jumped in, and locked all the doors. Her hands shook so badly she couldn't get the key in the ignition. In the backseat, Sophie gurgled and tried to pick up the book in her fat fists.

Oh God, what to do? Run, but where? How? Her best friend, Ava, lived in a tiny place with two other girls. She couldn't go there. Maybe a shelter? Leave Dallas, or the state of Texas altogether? Finally getting the key in, she started the car and got them on the road. She hurried home, watching her rearview mirror the entire time.

Was Dylan following them? How long had he been watching them? She needed the money from the sale of the trailer to make a new life for her and Sophie. Or pay lawyers if it came to a custody battle.

She'd thought she had more time, but she'd been wrong. She had to find a safe place to stay while selling the trailer. There was only one person Becky could think of who might be able to help—her boss, Lucinda Knight.

• • •

As his truck ate up the last miles toward home, Logan Knight refused to think about his deadline in three months. Or the wife he'd need to acquire to keep his acreage on the family ranch.

All he wanted was to get home, strip, and fall into bed. A couple days of peace and solitude would get his nightmares back under control, and then he'd be ready to tackle that contract with his father that he'd foolishly signed before heading off to boot camp almost twelve years ago.

Turning into the Knight Ranch, the headlights of his truck sliced through the inky darkness blanketing Texas's premier horse ranch. They also had cattle, but their reputation was in their competitive and working Quarter horses. Logan took the road leading north, heading to his land in the most secluded, rustic section. The moonlight poured through the trees, casting long shadows on the finished stables and making the just-framed cabins look like skeleton bones.

In the next three months, Logan was going to turn those bones into a full-fledged retreat for war veterans struggling to cope with PTSD. Camp Warrior Recovery was Logan's way of doing something that mattered. He supposed it was his way of atoning.

Without warning, the present faded away, replaced by the vivid image of those eight young girls, and the baby—oh God, the baby—all dead. Logan stopped his truck on the side of the road and rubbed his face, willing his one horrifying failure as a Marine to the back of his mind.

In seconds, the memory faded. He breathed a sigh of relief and pulled back onto the road. It was just a brief flash brought on by fatigue. Now that he was home, a few days alone and working on his retreat would level him out.

His three-bedroom house came into view, a dim light glowing in the huge front window. His cousin Lucinda was the only one who knew he was coming home. She must have been by to check on the place and stock his fridge. He owed her a steak dinner.

Once in the house, he toed off his boots, the tension melting from his muscles. Lucinda had left the light on beneath his over-the-range microwave, and judging from the illumination pouring down the hallway, his bedroom lamp. That soft glow drew him like a beacon. Striding across the wood floor, he headed down the hallway so ready to grab a shower and—

A low growl from the bedroom erupted into furious barking.

The hairs on the back of his neck sprang up. Adrenaline powered through him. What the hell was a dog doing in his house?

Quickly securing his weapon from his duffle bag, he swung into the doorway of his bedroom just as a something short and squat came barreling out. A set of determined teeth latched onto his jeans at his ankle, whipping back and forth. Ignoring the dog, he zeroed in on a woman scrambling off his bed. For a second, all he saw was long toned legs, then the tail of a blue shirt sliding around a luscious set of thighs. Dragging his gaze higher, the top buttons of the shirt were undone, gaping open to reveal full, ripe curves.

"Get out! I'm calling 911!"

Her voice snapped him out of his lust fog enough to see that she had a kid, a baby, cradled against her shoulder. Jesus, he had his gun in his hand; he could have shot them both. Fury rippled down his spine. "Do it. Tell the cops you're squatting in my house with a kid." He dragged in a breath to get control. "You're damned lucky I didn't shoot you."

The woman fumbled the phone, her eyes locked on the gun and color drained from her face. "Oh God. We have

Chapter Two

Becky stared at the text on her phone, and reminded herself that she couldn't kill her boss.

> *Trust me. You and Sophie are safer with Logan than anywhere else. This is for the best, even if Logan doesn't realize it yet.*

She didn't have much of a choice tonight. Plus, Lucinda had found a lawyer who would see her for a free consultation tomorrow. She really was helping. But Becky still wanted to yell at her. That scene with Logan had scared, embarrassed, and humiliated her. The man didn't want her in his house. Even worse, she was in the master bedroom. Shame added to the stew of discomfort.

After burping her sleeping daughter, Becky laid her in the second-hand, portable crib next to the massive wood framed bed. The room was a combination of rustic charm with beamed ceilings, warm-toned walls, and a stone fireplace that contrasted with the contemporary feel of huge windows lining one wall. Guilt banded around her lungs. She'd chosen the room because it had a nice area for Sophie's bed.

She'd not only invaded Logan's house, but she'd taken his room.

They couldn't stay in this room. It wasn't right. She dragged on some shorts; she'd embarrassed herself enough for one night. At the door, she glanced back at Jiggy plopped down on the floor by Sophie's bed. "Stay." Then she went into the hallway and closed the door.

At the same second the bathroom door opened, spilling out a billow of steam and a man wearing nothing except a towel loosely wrapped around lean hips. Above that was a rippled abdomen spreading into a muscular chest and shoulders that filled the doorway. On his left bicep he had a tattoo of a horse kneeling before a white cross draped with dog tags.

That tat tugged at her heart. He'd lost someone, and she understood how deep that pain went.

"Oh." The word squeaked out of her involuntarily. She was tall, nearly five ten, but she had to look up to see his unusual light green eyes that stood out against his darker skin and black hair.

"Need something?"

Even his voice was sexy, pitched low and oh-so-masculine. *Really?* After a year of her sex drive lying dormant, now her hormones noticed a man?

Stop staring like a moron and say something!

"I took your bedroom." A flush heated her skin. Where was all her beauty contestant poise and confidence?

He leaned against the doorjamb. "I noticed."

Was that towel around his waist sliding? A drop of water traveled down, tucking along his oblique muscles, over the jut of his hipbone, and vanishing into the knot of that terrycloth. "I want to give it back. Your room. I had no right to take it. I didn't know you were coming home, but still, I should have taken one of the other rooms. I'll just get our things and…" She turned, desperate to escape back into the room.

"Hey, easy there, sugar. You don't need to move rooms."

His calm confidence filled the hallway, easing her tension. "You're sure? Are you leaving again tomorrow or something? Lucinda said you travel for work." If he was leaving tomorrow, maybe he wouldn't mind letting her stay a more couple days since he wouldn't be here.

"I work for Once a Marine Security Agency, but I've taken a leave for a few months."

A leave squashed that idea, but she was intrigued by his job. "Security agency?" She couldn't help taking another eye-trip over his amazingly powerful body that looked custom-made to shield others. "Like bodyguarding?"

His grin tilted. "At times. We handle all kinds of private security and investigations."

"That's why you had the gun?"

Grim lines settled over his face. "Yes, but I don't make a habit of pulling it on an unarmed woman and her kid. I didn't know who was in my house or if they had a weapon."

"That's a relief. You scared the hell out of me."

His harsh look faded away. "The room is yours for a night or two."

Something was different about him from a half hour ago. Aside from his interesting state of undress, he was more relaxed and easygoing. More in command, both of himself and his home. Yeah, that was it.

He lowered his chin. "Lucinda would kill me if I let something happen to you. I'm in the business of security and protection, remember? You're perfectly safe in my house and on my land."

She'd bet if any man hurt Lucinda, Logan would protect his cousin. Glancing around, at anything but the powerful man taking up too much space in the hallway, the old and familiar envy reared up. It'd been a long day; she'd feel better if she got a few hours sleep. Forcing a light tone, she said, "Then I guess Sophie and I are safe." She wished to God that was true. "I'll make arrangements to leave as quickly as possible. Thank you for letting us stay here." She spun and reached for the doorknob.

"Becky."

"Yes?"

"I'm not good with kids. At all."

There it was again, that tension. It shadowed his eyes and added weight to his shoulders.

What did that mean exactly? But now wasn't the time to interrogate him. "I'll try to keep her quiet and out of your way."

• • •

Becky rubbed her clammy hands on her black slacks. She felt out of place sitting in this plush law office.

That was an all too familiar feeling after that scene with Logan last night. Once she finished here, she had to find a place for her and Sophie to stay. She couldn't impose on

Logan; he didn't want them there. Yet once he'd realized she was telling the truth, he'd been kind, going out of his way to reassure her that she and her baby were safe with him. While wearing nothing except that towel and some really sexy water droplets.

The sound of rustling papers dragged her attention from her thoughts.

Felicia Redding's blue eyes were battle-hardened, but not unkind, as she finished reading over the forms Becky had filled out.

"For Mr. Ridgemont to file for custody of Sophie he will first have to establish that he's the father. In Texas, when a baby is born to an unmarried couple, the law does not automatically recognize the biological father as a legal parent. Have you signed an Acknowledgement of Paternity naming Dylan Ridgemont as the baby's father since her birth?"

"No. Dylan was in prison when she was born. That's good, right?"

Felicia tapped her index finger on the polished surface of her desk. "It'll slow the process down while they get a court order for a paternity test. But until they have that, Mr. Ridgemont will have zero rights in regards to the child."

That gave her a little time. "Then he can file for custody?"

"Yes. Or he could file for visitation, but he'd be required to pay child support."

In that moment, she hated herself for saddling Sophie with Dylan as a father. She hadn't intended to get pregnant, but the end result was the same—Dylan was Sophie's father. Her daughter would pay a terrible price if she didn't find a way to keep her out of Dylan's hands. "I don't want support.

I just want Sophie to grow up safe and happy."

Felicia folded her hands on her desk. "You don't think she'd be safe with Mr. Ridgemont?"

"No, unless he handed her over to nannies or his parents or something. But that's not right. I'm Sophie's mom. Dylan attacked me when I was pregnant and put me in the hospital. Won't that be enough to keep him from getting custody?"

"It'll help, but the short answer is no." She leaned on her forearms. "Ms. Holmes, you need to grasp the reality here. Custody cases that go to court can be very expensive. I charge three hundred an hour for these cases. If Mr. Ridgemont brings the force of his family's legal counsel onto this case, it will be costly. We'll be buried in paperwork, and that will require countless hours of my paralegals' time as well as mine. I'd need a five thousand dollar retainer."

Desperation clogged her throat. She didn't have the money. Could she borrow against her trailer until she sold it? Glancing at her daughter sleeping in her car seat, determination rocketed through her. "I have a little time since he has to prove paternity. What about a restraining order for now?"

The lawyer picked up a pen and wrote something on a Post-it note. "Go to this website and download the protective order kit. You can do this yourself and save money. If you have any questions, call me and I'll walk you through it."

Grateful for the woman's help, she took the paper. "Thank you."

"Ms. Holmes, if Mr. Ridgemont wasn't one of Texas's richest families, I would direct you to some low income resources and you'd probably retain full physical custody of your daughter."

She went rigid from her jaw to her shoulders. "But?"

"If he makes a move to establish paternity, then he's in the process of going for custody. There's no benefit to him otherwise as he'll open himself up to pay child support."

That made sense.

"So if that happens, do whatever you have to in order to retain good counsel. It'll be an ugly fight. They have the money to do anything they need to, including having private investigators watching you."

Oh God. She had to find a way to get that money.

By the time she pulled up to Logan's house, exhaustion throbbed in her head and Sophie fussed incessantly. Taking the baby out of the car, she headed inside, grateful for the cool interior of the house.

Jiggy streaked out the door and down the steps, heading straight for the nearest tree. Becky set Sophie down in her carrier, trekked back out to the car to gather up the sewing she hoped to finish before work tonight, and called Jiggy. Once back inside, she changed Sophie and settled on the couch to feed her while researching the website the lawyer had given her. As the protective order forms downloaded, she wondered if she could get it filed and approved. Would a restraining order stop Dylan? Or would she just be provoking him into action? She was torn. What would keep them safe from Dylan?

Her boss thought Logan could.

Trust me. You and Sophie are safer with Logan than anywhere else.

He certainly looked capable enough even without the gun. The man exuded power, confidence, and an innate kindness that touched her. Becky had to admit, she had totally blindsided him by being in his house, yet he'd never once threatened her physical harm, let alone hurt her. And he'd looked pretty hot wearing that towel… She shook her head, getting off that train of thought.

The important thing was to stay safe while she figured out how to deal with Dylan. Her options were dwindling. Could she and Logan work out some trade for her and Sophie to stay there while she waited for the loan on the trailer to come through?

• • •

Logan had spent the day working on his land and thinking about Luce's suggestion—a temporary wife. He returned home, showered, and dressed, still turning it over in his mind.

His father had turned down every alternative, including Logan's offer to outright buy the land. Logan was screwed— he needed his land and home, but he couldn't have a wife who would depend on him and want children.

Children. Those dead girls, that baby…not going there. Kids were a trigger he avoided.

But a temporary wife? Becky was already here, and she appeared to be in trouble. These were special circumstances: either he married or he lost the land that meant everything to him. So if he had to deal with a baby for a few months…

His father had left him little choice. This strip of land was supposed to be his free and clear on his eighteenth birthday. But his old man was a manipulative bastard, determined to retain control over his son, and used the land to do it by adding a stipulation that Logan had to marry and live on the land by his thirtieth birthday or the land would revert to Brian Knight.

A temporary marriage meant he'd not only get what he wanted, but ultimately beat his father at his own game. And he could help out Becky while doing it. It was clear she was in some kind of trouble.

Luce's idea was gaining appeal. Logan headed out to the kitchen, determined to talk to Becky. Get to know her a little bit and see if his cousin was on to something.

Half way to the kitchen, a soft noise drew his attention to the floor. Baby Sophie lay on her tummy face-to-face with Jiggy. She arched her chest up and reached her tiny hand toward the dog's face.

Unease crept in at the sight of the baby. That was the complication. If it was just the woman, sure he could probably do it. But a baby? Such a fragile little person, anything could happen to her. He didn't want to be responsible for her safety.

The dog licked Sophie's waving fist. The baby gurgled and grinned, revealing toothless gums.

"Jiggy, not her hands or face." Becky stood at the island facing his open dining room and living room.

Pulling his attention from the baby relaxed some of his uneasiness. Becky had a black T-shirt on that set off her light hair and hugged her breasts. Temptation fisted in his belly, the same temptation that kept him awake thinking about the gorgeous woman in his bed. By morning, he'd convinced himself he'd exaggerated her beauty.

Wrong.

Even fully clothed, she was sizzling hot.

Stop staring, you moron. Dude, she stared back when you came out of the shower.

He ignored that voice of lust screaming in his brain. Going into the kitchen, he surveyed the half loaf of bread, jar of peanut butter, and small bunch withering grapes.

She lifted her gaze. "Hi."

It came out breathy, and her eyes warmed as her skin took on a dusky glow. Definitely not just him feeling this attraction. It took all his control not to look down and see if her nipples had pebbled, because if he looked...yeah, eyes on her face. "Hi, making a snack?"

"Dinner." She returned to her task. "We'll be out of your way in a few minutes. Well Sophie and I will. Is it okay if Jiggy stays here? I'll be back around midnight. I've fed him, he won't be any trouble."

Was it him making her nervous, or the charged air between them? "Sure, the dog can stay with me. Where are you going?"

"Work, but Sophie goes with me."

Right, she worked for Lucinda's cleaning company. Giving her some space, he went to the fridge, pulled out a cold bottle of beer then leaned against the counter. She took the baby with her to clean? Was that wise? Not his problem. What he needed to think about was firing up the grill and getting some dinner going. "Is that what you're eating for dinner?"

"Yes." Her shoulders stiffened as she dropped a couple slices of bread on a plate and picked up a knife. "I brought it with me."

Her defensiveness surprised him. Logan crossed the

room and lifted the jar. "What is this stuff?" He didn't even recognize the label. Must be an off-brand.

Becky tilted her chin up. "It's chunky. May I have it back please?"

"Don't you have to eat more than this?" She was feeding a kid.

She dropped her gaze. "Peanut butter works." Her stomach growled.

He'd made her uncomfortable when she was just trying to eat. Handing her the jar back, he lightened his tone. "Sure it does. I like peanut butter, but tonight I'm in the mood for steak. I'm going to fire up the grill and throw some on. Would you like to join me?"

She shook her head, her attention on her task. "Thanks for asking, but I need to get to work. This is faster and it's fine."

Logan caught himself inhaling her scent, reigniting his lust. His hands itched to touch her hair, see if it was as silky as it looked, and her skin as soft.

Whoa cowboy.

He reigned in the flash of desire. He was trying to get to know her and see if Lucinda's idea had merit, not take her to his bed. Would this attraction be a problem? Or something they could both enjoy? Logan took a long swallow of beer, determined not to let desire cloud his judgment.

Becky's scent faded as she went around the island, perched on a barstool, and took a bite of her sandwich.

He lowered his beer bottle. His lust took a backseat to the thought of her going hungry, or at least not eating enough. "Do you want jelly? I'm sure I have some." Cleaning was hard work. She needed more than peanut butter on crappy bread.

She shook her head.

Unable to stand it, Logan went to the fridge, got out the milk, and poured her a glass. "At least drink this."

Becky lifted her gaze, her eyes warring between suspicion and gratefulness. That expression twisted something in his stomach. It was that flicker of naked vulnerability backed up with steel determination. He pushed the glass toward her. "It's just milk. Drink it."

"I meant to buy some."

He put the carton away. "I can't drink all this. It'd be a waste for you to buy more."

"Still, I'll replace it when I leave." She set down her sandwich. "You left early this morning."

"Working on my land."

"Yeah? You mean the whole ranch? Or a part that's just yours?" She glanced out the slider. "This place looked huge when I drove in last night."

"I have roughly ten acres." That he was going to find a way to keep. "But the entire ranch is well over a hundred thousand acres."

Becky's hand holding her sandwich fell to the counter. "Wow, that's…wow. What do you do with all that land?"

"We breed and train horses, mostly Quarter for rodeo and to work. We're known for our horses and top-notch training. We have beef cattle, too. It's a huge operation with a massive staff, there's a lot of buildings and equipment to maintain."

"I can barely maintain my car." Remembering her sandwich, she took a bite.

Logan laughed. "Yeah, it's overwhelming." There was an

entire management team that, if his dad had his way, would one day be reporting to Logan. He didn't want that, never had.

Her eyes sparkled. "What's your favorite part?"

Easy answer. "Rehabilitating horses, especially abused or neglected ones, or horses that have been subjected to poor training techniques." There was nothing like getting a horse to trust him.

"Is that what you're doing while on leave from your job? Working with horses?"

"I'm going to turn this piece of land into Camp Warrior Recovery for veterans struggling with PTSD. Horses will be a part of the program."

Her eyes shimmered with interest. "Like a retreat or therapy?"

"Both." Involuntarily, his gaze went to the baby playing with the dog. Such a simple scene, one that should make him smile. Instead, he worried it would trigger his claustrophobia, and the need to get out of the house and away from the kid. Right now, he was level, able to control his anxiety.

Not wanting to get into that with Becky, he shifted the subject. "I'll be pitching in on the ranch, too." He didn't mind helping, but he wasn't stepping into his dad's shoes. Not only did he not want it, but rightfully that job should go to Abby, his half-sister. She lived and breathed the ranch, loved it with the passion that running a ranch like this required. But their old-fashioned, sexist father didn't agree. He demanded that his one and only son take over. Becky's voice rescued him from his thoughts.

"That brings me to something I was hoping to talk to you about. Can we work something out so Sophie, Jiggy, and

I can stay a week or two? I'm working on getting a loan and a restraining order—"

"Hold up." Logan set down his beer. How much trouble was she in? His sense of self-preservation screamed, *Be smart, don't get involved*. His protective instincts, however, kicked the shit out of his self-preservation. "Tell me about this restraining order. Against whom and for what?"

She glanced over at her baby making noise and drooling all over one of Jiggy's paws.

"My ex-boyfriend."

Logan returned his attention to Becky. "He's your baby's father?" So she hadn't been married. He didn't like the guy already.

"Yes. The short version is that we dated in college. When I realized I was pregnant, I told him while we were in his truck." She looked down at the remainder of her sandwich.

He knew he wasn't going to like this story and he steeled himself. "He didn't take it well?"

"No. He was furious." She took a deep breath, lifted her eyes. "That part's not important."

Oh, he thought it was, but he held his silence.

"He was yelling at me, not watching where he was going." She turned to gaze out the sliding glass door. "He hit a man. I can still remember the awful sound."

That…damn. Logan hadn't seen that coming. He needed to know what he was dealing with. "What happened?"

"He drove away, leaving the bleeding man lying on the road." She stared down at her fisted hand. "I turned Dylan in. He took a plea deal and was supposed to get a few years. But he's out already. He cornered me in the parking lot of a grocery store, threatened to finish the job with me. He knew details about my life, like which office I clean on any given night, that my mom died, even that Jiggy pees on the FOR SALE sign in front of my trailer."

The words were pouring out in huge waves, drowning him in a sea of information. He tried to hone in on one problem at a time. "What did he mean by finish the job with you?"

"When I called 911 to report that we'd hit that man... he was mad."

"He attacked you?" Okay, now he was pissed. Logan went to the sink and dumped out the last half of his beer. Mixing alcohol with his rage would shatter his hard-won control. Instead, he grabbed a bottle of water.

"Dylan wanted me to confess to driving the truck, and get him off the hook."

He filed that name and went on. "You didn't change your story?"

"No." She glanced at her watch. "I have to go to work, but I'm afraid of him and his lawyers. His family is very rich and he said he was filing for custody of Sophie. I'm scared to stay in my trailer right now. I'm hoping you and I can work something out for a week or two."

"Like what?"

"I can clean the house and do your laundry. I'm good at sewing if you need any of your clothes repaired."

Ah, she wanted to do a trade. He could see why his cousin liked Becky. The girl had some pride. "You don't have to do that." If she was in trouble, he wasn't going to make her work for a place to stay.

Her hand tightened around the glass of milk. "I want to. I can cook, too. I'm not great, but I can make a few things."

When he shut the fridge and turned, additional tension had compressed her pretty mouth. "It's that important to you?" Or was she still upset rehashing her troubles?

"Yes."

No hesitation or coyness; she really did want to earn her way. "Why?" When Logan was in Dallas, most people recognized him as one of the Knights from the Knight Ranch. Somehow, he always ended up picking up checks. The exception to that were his Marine buddies, Sienna, and now Becky.

She picked a grape off the stem. "I don't want to take advantage of you. I know Lucinda put you in a bad position, and you obviously aren't the kind of man to throw a woman and baby out."

This might work out in his favor. It would give him time to get to know Becky. Maybe they would work out an even bigger deal.

The temporary marriage kind of deal.

Chapter Three

Becky leaned closer, desperate for Logan to agree to let her and Sophie stay in his house for a week or two. That would give her some time to figure out her options. If she got that loan, she could hire the lawyer. Would a restraining order keep Dylan from coming after her? Or Sophie? She needed time to sort it all out.

"Do we have a deal?"

He set his water on the counter. "Yes."

The man was too sexy for his own good, and for her peace of mind. That she could handle, but that whole thing about him building a camp to help vets with PTSD pulled at her heartstrings and stirred a longing that went deeper than desire. But she needed to keep her mind on their trade. "Thank you. I won't be home until midnight, but I can start in the morning. I'll wash all the sheets, remake the beds, and move my stuff out of your room. Just leave a list of anything specific you want me to do." She picked up her sandwich, determined to finish it before she left.

"I have one condition though."

Wariness mixed with confusion. "What kind of condition?"

He flattened his hands on the island counter. "I'll agree to you doing housekeeping chores in exchange for room and board. But that means you help yourself to my food or anything in my kitchen."

Not only was he sexy, but he was generous without making her feel bad. Did he have any idea what that meant to her? "I have food."

He glanced at the cheap peanut butter and cardboard bread she'd left on the counter. A second later, he leaned forward, his eyes catching the setting sun, turning them a darker shade of green. "Not negotiable. You don't like being indebted and I respect that. I don't like eating steak while a woman in my home eats a sandwich."

"That really bothers you?"

"Sugar, it annoys the shit out of me."

A laugh spilled out before she caught it. His bluntness worked for her; her respect for him notched up. Logan wasn't a spoiled rich boy. "We can't have that. I'll eat your food."

He leaned one forearm on the counter, and touched her wrist, holding the remainder of her sandwich. "Then I just have one question."

His fingers lightly brushed over her wrist bone, shooting tingling sensations through her. "What?" Hearing the slight catch in her voice, she fought a wince.

"Forget the sandwich. How do you want your steak cooked?"

For a second, she wanted nothing more than to let him

cook dinner for her. *Idiot.* Here she was on the run, hiding from Dylan, had a baby to care for and she fell into instant lust. Forcing a smile, she said, "Rain check. I have to get to work."

• • •

Friday afternoon, he pulled up to his house with a twinge of disappointment. He was going to have to bail on dinner with Becky. Barely four days home, and he'd been summoned to his dad's house for a mandatory family dinner.

That Logan had expected. What surprised him was his regret at not being able to eat with Becky. In a few days' time, they'd fallen into a routine. He went out and worked on his land and searched for more stock to fill his stable. Becky did her thing around the house, taking care of her baby, and doing the agreed upon chores. Once Logan got home and showered, they had dinner that Becky cooked. Then Becky went to work.

A temporary marriage could work between them. They liked each other, but the sexual chemistry—yeah that could be an issue. Still, they were adults, and Logan fully understood the word no. If she didn't want to complicate things with sex, he'd deal with it.

It's only for a few months.

And the kid?

Logan grimaced. He'd be gone all day, beginning before dawn and coming home around dinner, and sometimes he'd have to go back out after that. Between his camp and the ranch, he'd be spending most of his waking hours working. He could handle the baby. Had to. He wasn't letting his dad get the land. And he liked the idea of helping Becky secure custody. That was a sore spot with him, given that his own mom had lost custody of him.

Decided, he headed into the house.

Jiggy raced to the door, wiggling all over. "Dude, man up." Yet he squatted down and petted the little guy while thinking about what he'd say to her.

"You're home early." Becky walked out from the hallway.

Logan's hand froze on the dog's neck. His body twanged as he drew his gaze up her bare calves and toned thighs to her black shorts. The waistband rested on her hip bones leaving a strip of her light colored skin bare. It took him long seconds to get enough brainpower to work out why her stomach was exposed. She'd tied a knot in the white T-shirt. He didn't care what her reason for doing it was, he fully approved.

"I was cleaning windows and didn't expect you home yet." She fidgeted with the knot resting at the curve of her waist. "The shirt got in my way." The material released from the coil and fell around her hips.

Straightening, he grinned. "Not complaining."

"You were staring."

True. How could he not? She brought out the sexy in window washing. But was she flustered or upset? She'd relaxed in the last few days. Logan circled the big chair and couch to stop in front of her. He was close enough to see the tiny green speckles hidden in her brown eyes. "You stared at me when I was in a towel." Not that he'd minded.

She rolled her eyes. "Only because you were practically posing."

"I don't pose."

"You leaned against the doorjamb and flexed. I know all about posing, cowboy. You. Were. Posing."

Logan was entranced by her confident teasing. She was also right, but it'd take a superheated branding iron to get him to admit it. "That so? And what makes you so experienced? Do you strike a lot of poses while cleaning offices? Or at play dates with your daughter?"

Becky's chin shot up and amusement tugged at her full lips. "Is that a challenge?"

His talk with her could wait a few minutes. This was too much fun. "Oh yeah." What would she do? He had to fight the familiar urge to touch her cheek and stroke all her skin to learn the angles and planes that made her face so interesting. Becky made him laugh one minute, then turned him inside out the next. She had a sweet sexiness he was coming to crave. Being around her chased out the darkness in him.

"Accepted. Stand back, I'm going to need room to work."

Did she now? Logan moved back to the table, leaving Becky in the walkway between the table and living room. "Have at it, darlin'." He leaned his ass against the thick table, crossing one booted foot over the other. She looked cute in that hot girl next door way with her ponytail, loose T-shirt, and shorts.

Becky kicked off her worn athletic shoes, pulled the ends of the T-shirt up, and retied it.

Logan sucked in a breath. That flash of taut skin stretched across her slight curve of a belly made him swallow. His view was disrupted when Becky pulled the band out of her hair, leaned over at the waist and shook her head. Then she flipped her hair up and it fell around her in streams of wild honey.

His heart skipped a beat. What happened to that sweet, slightly embarrassed girl? This woman was…wow. The transformation stunned him. He opened his mouth to say something when she started to move.

The words lodged in his chest. Becky held her head high, threw her shoulders back, outlining her full breasts beneath that shirt. Her hips rolled with sinuous grace as she glided across the floor on gorgeous long legs. Once she reached the kitchen island, she stopped as if she hit the end of a runaway. Putting one hand on her hip, she arched her body in a provocative pose and flashed him a dazzling smile. She stayed that way for several seconds.

Logan jerked upright, his pulse galloping. Lust and need coiled low in his groin. It took everything he had to stay where he was. He wanted to touch her. Hell, he wanted to strip her naked and discover every inch of the woman who just a few minutes ago had been self-conscious about having her stomach exposed. Now she was brazenly working it. Which was the real Becky? He hoped it was both — sweet and spicy.

She dropped her arm, sliding into an agile turn, and creating ripples in her golden blond hair that couldn't be an accident. She walked back.

Right at him.

Her breasts bounced, hips swayed, and that smile never once lost its glorious perfection. Total high-fashion model and girl next door rolled into one breath-stealing, hard-on inducing package. She coasted to a stop when her bare toes nearly touched the tips of his boots.

The sultry scent of honeysuckle wafted from her. Tilting

her head up she said, "With more than ten years in beauty pageants, I know posing when I see it."

Sweat popped out beneath his shirt and his dick swelled. It wasn't just the sensuality of her walk and pose, but the way she'd just put him in his place. "You win." His voice came out low and rough. For days they'd been dancing around this desire between them. He could almost see the streaks of electricity arcing between them.

Her flawless smile melted, and her gaze locked onto his. "What's my prize?"

Those three breathy words fried his brain until all that remained was fiery need. Logan buried his hands in her heavy, silken hair. "A kiss." Something he was supposed to do niggled at his brain while he waited to see if she'd say no, but he couldn't focus on it. Didn't want to. All that mattered was Becky and he stroked the soft skin of her cheek.

The pulse at the base of her throat fluttered, and her full lips parted. She leaned into him.

That simple gesture of her trust pulled him to her with a magnetic force. Her warm breath merged with his as he brushed his lips over her soft full mouth, catching her taste with the lightest touch of his tongue. The contact ripped away the veneer he kept ruthlessly in place.

The raw, damaged man in him exploded to the forefront. Logan wrapped an arm around her waist, that strip of bared skin branded his arm. He lifted and hauled her against his body. Her breasts pressed against his chest. He searched her face. No fear there, only desire turning this girl-next-door sweetheart into his brazen beauty.

Her tongue darted out, wetting her full lips like an invitation then retreating.

Buzzing ramped up in his ears, a need so visceral he could actually hear it. That mouth, oh yeah, he wanted Becky's mouth, and the moans he hoped to entice from her. Lowering his head, he brushed his mouth over her damp, soft lips. Her taste teased him mercilessly, powering a fierce hunger to delve in and discover every sweet secret of this woman in his arms. Determined to keep control, to give her the best first-prize kiss in the history of kissing, he licked a slow sweep over the tantalizing bow of her bottom lip.

Not enough, he had to have more.

Capturing her lip, he gently sucked. Then he left her mouth, kissing across her silky skin, over the curve of her jaw to the sensitive spot by her ear and confessed the truth:

"Losing never felt or tasted so damned good."

• • •

A tiny warning sounded in Becky's head.

Are you doing it again? Jumping too fast in your desperate need to be loved?

But she'd never experienced this intensity. Her heart pounded, her nipples pebbled against Logan's slab of a chest while his arms held her securely. The roaring in her head drowned out that thin voice of caution. Latching onto his shoulders, she turned her mouth to his.

His lips covered hers, and he licked deep into her mouth, exploring and commanding. She kissed him back, tangling her tongue with his, the rough wet texture shivering through her. She'd never get enough.

A low growl of approval rumbled in his chest, teasing her nipples. Tiny shocks shot straight down to her core. A hot ache bloomed there, throbbing. Spreading his hand over her lower back, he stroked his thumb across her skin and her nerves lit on fire. That ache intensified. She mewled, trying to get closer.

Logan slid a hand over her hip, hooking her thigh over his hip. She shuddered, the feel of his hand like a sensual brand searing through her pants.

He rolled his hips, and the hard ridge of his erection pressed against her core. Hot streaks of wild pleasure blasted her nerve endings. All the while he kissed her, his mouth consuming hers. Every part of Logan filled, surrounded, and cradled her, coaxing pleasure and need higher and higher. Unable to catch her breath, she broke the kiss.

Too much, too soon. She'd practically climbed up Logan, riding him. Reality crashed over her with hot waves of shame. She'd only known him for days and acted like a...

Gold-digging whore.

The accusation from Dylan's parents screamed in her head. Scrambling out of his arms, she backed up, desperate to escape.

• • •

Confused by the sudden shift in Becky, Logan released her. "Hey, what's wrong?" God, had he hurt her?

She shook her head, refusing to look at him. "I...uh... Sophie's awake." She whipped around, heading to the hallway.

He didn't hear anything, but he sure as hell could see the humiliation burning her face. "Becky, wait."

"I can't." She vanished into the bedroom she shared

with Sophie and shut the door.

Logan followed; he couldn't let her go like this. What had happened that caused her to run, her face stained with embarrassment? Leaning his forehead against the closed door, he said softly, "Becky, sweetheart, talk to me."

Nothing. The utter silence on the other side of the door tore at his heart. Jesus, could he have screwed this up anymore? He'd come home wanting to discuss helping each other out with a temporary marriage. Instead he kissed her, and obviously crossed some line, upsetting her.

"My father is expecting me at his house for dinner, but I'm not leaving you unless you talk to me. Tell me you're okay." Now wasn't the time to discuss anything else.

"Go to your dad's."

He let out a sigh, part relief that she'd at least spoken to him, and part regret. He didn't want to leave her. "I can cancel." Right now, he didn't give a shit about his dad. He needed to find out what had upset her and fix it. "I'll cook us dinner and—"

"Please go. I'm fine. I just need some space."

Logan leaned back against the wall. What should he do? Everyone needed space, he understood that all too well.

"I'll go, but I'll be home later tonight if you want to talk."

Chapter Four

The entire time Logan was getting ready, driving to the house, and even while standing in his father's home office, all he could think about was Becky. That kiss…Jesus, he'd completely lost his head. It was Becky—young, beautiful, so alive and real that she tugged hard at the jaded ugliness swimming around in him. So sweet and trusting, he'd wanted nothing more than to give her pleasure and feel like a man. A whole decent man who was worthy of touching her.

Not a walking time bomb that had to fight to keep his demons leashed.

Touching Becky, kissing her, and feeling her body against his eased that constant low-grade anxiety brewing in him. Until he'd seen that shattered look on her face. Then she'd all but run from him.

"Are you listening?"

Logan turned from the window to face his father sitting behind the massive mahogany desk in his study. The years of hard work, hard drinking, and just being a hard-ass were taking a toll on Brian Knight. At forty-nine, he had craggy lines digging into his harsh face and more gray than black hair. "Are you saying something new?" Okay, maybe the hard-ass trait was genetic.

Brian rose and dropped his knuckles down on the desktop. "You've got some woman holed up in the house you're currently using."

Ah, the spies on the ranch were working overtime. "It's my house." The one he'd built on the land he would get the title to one way or another.

"If you grow up and assume your responsibilities. You're almost thirty and still acting like…*her*."

"No surprise there. She is my mother." Nothing like twisting that knife in the old man. Brian didn't like the reminder that he'd fallen in love with the *wrong sort of girl*, resulting in Logan. For the first eight years of his life, Logan hadn't even known what his father looked like. Hadn't really cared. Until the day his mother was arrested.

He clamped down on the anger threatening to erupt.

"Get that woman off my land. And it's still *my* land until you fulfill the contract. You won't find a decent woman to marry while keeping a bimbo in your house."

Logan crossed to the desk and slapped his hands down. Face to face, he kept his voice low and calm. "Her name is Becky. She works for Luce and is renting a room from me." Doing chores was the same as paying rent. "I have zero tolerance for your judgmental bullshit." He'd learned a long time ago not to back down from his father.

"And I have zero tolerance for your ungrateful rebellion. You are my son."

Not hers were the unspoken words hanging between them. No matter how much he tried, Brian couldn't break Indigo's influence on Logan. After all, he'd spent his early years traveling with her across the United States as she sang in club after club. Then his father had ruined it all, got custody of Logan, and dragged him to this house where Logan was stifled and claustrophobic.

But Logan had found his place on the land down by the pond. That piece of wild beauty and tranquil fishing became Logan's solace. When he was a kid, thrown into a family where he never really belonged, that land had been his one comfort. The one thing he knew was his—his mother had made sure of it. And later, when the nightmares and flashbacks about forcing himself into that tiny mud house and finding a bloodbath of dead children threatened to consume him, Logan discovered the land and his house calmed and centered him. Building the Camp Warrior Recovery gave him a purpose to keep living.

"I want that woman gone."

Logan stared at his father across the desk from him. "Do you? Sign over my land and she'll be gone tonight." His father wouldn't do it, but if he did, Logan would put Becky in a safe place.

Problem was, he liked her in his house. He caught his almost-frown. Now wasn't the time to think about Becky.

"You signed the contract. You will marry and live on the land, or it reverts back to me on your birthday." Shoving back from the desk, he crossed his arm. "I did my best to toughen you up after *she* tried to turn you into a damned long-haired hippie."

Logan narrowed his eyes. "Must have worked. I was a

Marine for a decade."

"You followed orders. Any grunt can do that. The Knight men give orders. So here's how it's going to be. First, you marry a decent woman and start producing heirs. You'll quit that job and I'll teach you how to run the ranch." Brian strode to the sideboard and poured out a glass of scotch. "The real working horse ranch, not some hippie commune bullshit for dropouts who can't handle life. Men do their duty without complaint, whether it's to their country or their family business. They don't run around looking for pity and handouts because life takes a piss on them. They handle it."

And Logan wasn't handling it in his father's opinion. Getting help for PTSD made him less than a man. "We're done here." He pivoted with military precision, back ramrod straight and breathing to keep his fury contained.

"Running away like her?"

The taunt spun him.

Brian lifted his chin, sensing victory. "All you have to do is marry to get that land you love so much. Can't even do that much?"

Oh he could. And would, if he could get Becky to agree. "I'll marry and get my land."

• • •

Just after midnight, and struggling with despair and exhaustion, Becky left her sleeping baby in the bedroom and took the dreaded envelope with her out to the kitchen. Earlier tonight at work, she'd been served the subpoena ordering her to present Sophie for a DNA testing to establish whether or not Dylan was her biological father. He was really going to try to take Sophie away from her.

Too many worries clashed in her head, but one thing was abundantly clear—she had to get the retainer for the lawyer. Holding up her right hand, she eyed her mom's wedding rings. They were all she had left, but she had to sell them.

Images flashed in her head. Her parents laughing in the kitchen. Her father reading to her. Tyler teaching her how to make a paper airplane. Her memories jumped to that last fatal day, her mom screaming, the police holding her back as the firemen fought the flames...

Stop it. Reliving the past wouldn't help her keep Sophie out of Dylan's hands. She needed a plan; sell the rings, and see if that would at least get the lawyer started until the trailer sold.

Right now, she needed to eat something. Opening the freezer, the blast of cool air felt good. She eyed the chocolate chip ice cream still sealed with the plastic ring. That might ease the burn in her stomach.

Becky picked up the carton, shut the door, and almost screamed. "Logan!"

"Midnight snack?"

Her mouth dried while her pulse beat in her ears. Dressed in nothing but black pajama bottoms and bronzed skin, he instantly dominated the large kitchen. His rumpled black hair and dark-shadowed jaw screamed sexy danger. "What?"

He uncoiled, taking the carton from her hand and held it up. "Hungry?" His eyebrows lowered, and concern etched around his mouth. "Did you eat dinner before you went to work?"

All her earlier shame and humiliation at practically

climbing up him when he'd kissed her flooded back. "No time. I was just…I'm not that hungry after all. I'll get out of your way." She couldn't face him yet and spun to go around the other side of the island.

"Becky, wait. Please sit with me and have some ice cream. I won't touch you, I just want to talk."

His voice, God, it was like silky warm melted chocolate sliding over her skin. She couldn't hide from him in his own house. Time to suck it up. "Okay."

They worked together to serve the ice cream, then settled at the bar. Becky dug in, letting the cold, sweet dessert wash away the taste of fear and worry. She and Logan had eaten several meals together, and the familiarity of it soothed her. She glanced over at him. "Did I wake you?"

"I was awake. Thinking about you."

"Me?" Sitting here with him now in the soft light that held back the night, the room felt small and intimate. "Good or bad thoughts?"

"Both. That kiss was all good, until I pushed you too far, too fast, and you ran as if you had to escape me." He set his spoon down. "I don't want you to feel like you have to run from me."

"I wasn't running from you." She studied her bowl, fishing out the bite with the most chocolate chips. He made it so easy to talk to him. "I was ashamed of myself."

Logan swiveled, his attention fully on her. "Why?"

She took a breath. "It's never been like that before. Another minute or two and I would have lost it and had a—" Crap, she needed to engage the filter between her thoughts and mouth.

He leaned on his forearm. "The word is orgasm. And it's

just you and me sitting here, no one judging us. You can talk to me."

The truth spilled out of her. "I've confused sex and love in the past. It's kind of a pattern for me." For years she'd dreamed of that perfect family and home. She didn't need her college psychology classes to tell her she was subconsciously trying to replace what she'd lost as a little girl. With the way Logan made her feel so much so fast...yeah...too easy to confuse an experienced lover with a man truly caring.

Logan took a breath. "I like you, but I'm not going to fall in love with you."

"No!" *Oh my God.* "I know that. I didn't think you cared, I was just embarrassed and mad that I lost control, thinking with my hormones and not my brain." She bit off her words. Not so easy to talk now. "Can we talk about something else?"

"Not until you look at me."

Becky forced her eyes up.

His gaze captured hers and he leaned forward. Not touching her, but so close it felt like there was only the two of them in the world right now. "You're a beautiful woman with normal, healthy desires. You allowing me to give you pleasure? If we're both okay with it, then there's not a damn thing wrong with that."

It wasn't just his voice hypnotizing her, it was the way he surrounded her without touching her. His thighs were spread on either side of her knees, his face close enough to see his pupils were slightly dilated, and she could smell the clean scent of his soap and that richer male scent. It all wrapped around her, relaxing her reservations. "It sounds so simple."

"It is. There's enough complicated shit in the world. And

all kinds of bad shit. Don't let anyone take sex away from you. Sometimes, that's all we have left."

Becky had never heard anything as sad as that. She could see a barren desolation in his eyes. Unable to resist, she covered his hands with hers. "You've seen bad stuff." And suffered for it. If he was building a camp to help PTSD vets, then it was a safe guess that he dealt with it himself.

He went rigid. "Ten years in the Marines. I've seen and done things that I don't want you or any civilian I know to see." He looked away, his eyes losing focus. "Friends of mine died to make damn sure you never will."

Without thinking, she touched his tattoo. Its simplicity was heartbreaking—a majestic horse going to a knee before the cross with the dog tags. "This is for them? Your friends who died?"

"Yes."

"You don't force a horse like that to his knee." She stroked over the ink, as if she could soothe that horse, and Logan's wounded soul. "He gives that honor freely to one who died for his country. I can't think of a more fitting tribute from you." She forced herself to stop touching those haunting markings. "I'm sorry."

He nodded. "I chose to go in the Marines, and I'd do it again knowing full well what I'd face. I'd just do some things better if I had the chance."

His bravery and commitment touched her so deeply, her arms ached to hold him. Instead, she squeezed his hands.

Logan honed in on her fingers. He eased a thumb over the rings she wore on her right hand. "Wedding rings?" His eyes lifted to hers.

"My mother's. I need to sell them." Even the words felt

like a betrayal.

"Luce said your mother just passed?"

"A little over a month ago. I don't want to sell them." She bit her lip against a fresh wave of grief.

"Then why are you?"

She leaned past him and picked up the envelope. "I was served this tonight. It's a court order compelling a DNA test to establish that Dylan is Sophie's father."

"He's going after custody."

"I can't let him win. My loan hasn't come through yet, and I need to come up with a retainer for my lawyer. I should get enough from the rings." She swallowed a lump. Crying wouldn't help; she had to be strong.

He eased back from her. "Your ex is Dylan Ridgemont, his family owns Ridgemont Communications. They are wealthy and powerful."

The change in him threw her off balance. "Yes." Wait… "Did I tell you his last name?"

"No. I reviewed the background check Once a Marine Security Agency did on you when Luce hired you."

Uneasiness stiffened her spine. "Lucinda gave you that? I thought it was confidential."

"I work for Once a Marine. I also own part of Luce's business, so I have the right to see it."

What was going on here? The earlier warmth in him had cooled. "Is there a problem?"

He relaxed marginally. "You're smart enough to know there's a big problem with you going up against the Ridgemonts."

She took a breath. "I have to fight. Dylan didn't want Sophie, he told me to get rid of her." She closed her eyes as those awful moments in the truck screamed in her head. But this wasn't about her anymore. "I'm going to fight. She's my daughter and I'm not giving her up. She doesn't deserve to pay for my mistake of saddling her with Dylan as a father."

"Did you get the restraining order?"

Becky twisted the rings. "No. I filled out the paperwork, but I worried I'd just provoke him if I had him served with a restraining order."

Logan regarded her for a few seconds. "I pulled your background to find out more about you before I decided to approach you with a deal."

It took her a second to absorb the meaning of his words. "A deal for what?"

"A way for us to help each other out, and you won't have to sell your mom's rings."

"How?" She had no idea what Logan was worth, but she couldn't have anything he wanted.

"I need a temporary wife. Marry me for a few months, and I'll help you keep custody of your daughter."

• • •

Becky couldn't have heard him right. No way. "Marry you?"

"Yes. I need a wife until my thirtieth birthday in a little under three months."

"I…why?"

Logan leaned back against the island, stretching his long legs out in front of him. "I signed a contract with my father. If I'm not married by my thirtieth birthday, I lose my land."

Becky glanced around the kitchen, dining room, and living area. "This land you're building your camp on?"

"Yes."

Conflicting emotions rolled through her. "You're not exactly sharing information here. Yet you looked at my background."

He propped a foot on the rung of the stool. "How about we start with this. I'm not in the Ridgemonts' category, but I'm rich enough on my own—without my family's money—to pay your lawyers, as well as yours and Sophie's expenses. You can quit work to focus on being a mom and fighting for your girl."

"Marine pay must be awesome."

His mouth curved. "Not even close, sugar, but being a Knight opened doors for me, and I invested the money I didn't spend on the land very well. Add to that the power of the Knight name, and marrying me will make it harder for a judge to take Sophie from you. We will look and act like a stable family."

"Look and act?"

"Not only for Sophie, but for my family as well. This isn't a joke to me. I want my land, and I won't let my father win."

A chill dripped down her spine. For the first time, she saw the absolute hard-ass in him. The man who could kill, and no doubt had. "Do you hate your father?"

"It's complicated."

She lifted a brow. "Speak slowly and use small words. If I concentrate real hard, I might be able to understand."

"Funny. And a smart mouth."

"You're being secretive and evasive."

"Military trained."

"Pageant trained. We can do this all night. But if you want me to consider this wild scheme of yours, I need to know a little about you."

Logan cracked a grin. "Tough girl in a pretty package, huh?"

"Same goes for you."

Logan rolled his eyes. "Now you're just being mean. I'm not pretty."

"Suck it up and start talking."

He took a breath, expanding his shoulders and chest. "It's like this. Until I was eight years old, all I knew about my father was his name and that he owned a ranch in Texas."

"Did he know about you?"

"Yes. But I was a part of his life he desperately wanted to forget. So I spent those years on the road with my mother. Her name is Indigo White. My father met her when she was singing in a club. They fell in love and married. Very quickly, Mom figured out that she hated being married and trapped on a ranch. She took off when she was a few months pregnant and never looked back."

His flat voice contrasted with the tension in his jaw and neck. Logan didn't like telling this story. "So what changed when you were eight?"

"My stepmother, Pricilla, had some female issue that ended her ability to have more kids. I have two half sisters, but no other boys. My father needed me. But my mother wasn't going to give me up willingly, so he had her arrested on possession charges."

"Drugs?"

"The police found marijuana in the tour bus."

"Was it your mother's?"

"She denies it. I was eight, I don't know. But my father went after custody and won. An eight-year-old living on a barely running tour bus, sleeping on couches in the back of clubs while Indigo performed did not impress the judge. She lost all rights except some supervised visitation."

"You were right, it's complicated. Why did your dad need a son?"

"To inherit the ranch. A Knight always inherits the ranch."

"But you have two sisters. Aren't they Knights?"

"Until they marry. Girls are notoriously unstable that way."

"Wow. That's incredibly archaic and chauvinistic." And here she'd been a little jealous of Logan with his beautiful home on his family's land. But still... "Can't you talk to him? You're his son. Maybe he didn't have you those first years, but he must love you now."

"I don't know what the old man feels. But I know this... somewhere in that huge custody battle, my mother stopped fighting. She made a deal with my dad that he'd deed a certain amount of land to me on my eighteenth birthday so I would always have a home."

Becky's stomach dropped. "She gave you up?" After having him for eight years? How could she?

"She was going to lose. Indigo knew it and tried to wrangle something for me, not for herself." Logan looked up at the ceiling. "I think that was her way of making sure I'd know she cared even when she was forced to give me away." Logan turned, his gaze frozen. "That manipulative bastard followed the agreement, he deeded me the land but only if I signed the contract agreeing to his additional terms."

"What does he want?"

"For me to marry, have sons, and take over the ranch.

If I'm not married and living on the ranch by the time I'm thirty, the deed to the land reverts to him." Logan swiveled his head, shadows sucked the light out of his gaze. "I'm not letting him win this. I'm going to beat him at his own game."

"You don't want to get married some day? Have a family?"

"I can't. No kids."

She laid her hand on the slab of granite that passed for his arm.

He shook his head, cutting off her words. "Not going there, Becky. Don't ask. This marriage will be temporary, a business deal. I'll have my lawyer draw up a contract. We'll live here together until I secure my land. During that time, I'll take care of all your expenses, including the lawyer to fight for Sophie. Anything your baby needs, I'll provide." His eyes shadowed. "But you care for her. I can't."

She didn't point out that others might find that odd. If he married Becky, wouldn't he care for her daughter, too? Wasn't that what she'd need to convince a judge of to keep her baby?

"Once we both get what we want, we'll divorce and I'll give you a settlement that will be yours to do with as you please. Buy a house, open a business."

Her thoughts churned at the possibilities. If this worked, she'd have her baby and could finish her nursing degree. Make a real future for her and Sophie. Flutters of hope bubbled in her stomach. An hour ago she'd been desperate, but now Logan was offering her a lifeline that sounded too good to be true. "What's the catch?"

"There's no catch. We just have to make it look real. My father can't be suspicious or he'll dig until he finds the truth."

She stared at her hands, thinking. Could she do this? Could Logan? Should they? "It seems like an underhanded thing to do. We'd be lying to your family and everyone."

"Think of the payoff. As my wife, with us providing a stable life in a two-parent home for Sophie, and the power of my family name and money, you'll get custody of Sophie. Isn't she your priority?"

Her morals had a serious collusion with her priorities. "I'll think about it."

But if she wanted to keep her daughter, what choice did she have?

Chapter Five

"As your lawyer, I'm advising you not to sign this." Brody Harper slapped three copies of the contract down on the table outside the judge's chambers.

"Noted." Logan handed a copy to Becky. Her hand was icy cold, matching her pale face. Not exactly a glowing bride. But then, this wasn't exactly the wedding most girls dreamed of. For instance, most brides didn't wear a black sweater, mouthwatering jeans, and a pair of cowboy boots. Between the way that sweater clung to her full breasts and— *Focus.* "You sure you don't want your own lawyer to look this over?"

"No." She scanned the pages, reading with a singular intensity.

"You need a lawyer." Her friend, Ava, looked over Becky's shoulder, her eyes hard. "Make sure he's not trying to screw you outside the bedroom."

Becky whipped around, putting her body between him

and her friend. "Don't start. This deal is between me and Logan."

"No it's not. My goddaughter is involved, and that means I will be all over his fine ass if he hurts you or Sophie."

Brody rounded on him. "You're trusting Spandex Barbie here with inside knowledge of this deal? Are you insane? If your father finds out—"

"Whoa." Becky spun again, her furious eyes sliding past Logan to bore a hole in Brody. "Don't you dare question my friend's loyalty."

Brody puffed out his chest. "Hey, I'm bound by confidentiality. What's she bound by? Besides Lycra?"

Logan couldn't tear his gaze from Becky. The transformation stunned him. Her beautiful Bambi-sweet eyes narrowed with rage. Her shoulders jacked up, hands fisted, and angry energy crackled around her. "Friendship. Ava won't betray me or Sophie. Just like if she were to kill a lawyer, I'd help her hide the body."

"Her?" Brody threw a thumb in Ava's direction. "What's she going to do, kill me with hairspray?"

"That shit's flammable, genius." Ava stepped up so she was toe-to-toe with Brody. "A can of hairspray and a lighter equals a flamethrower."

Logan lifted his brow at Becky. "This is your best friend?"

"Look who's talking. Tell me this guy doesn't try cases in front of a jury? He has the charm of a horse's ass."

He fought a grin. "You'd really help her hide the body?"

"In a heartbeat, but I might need to borrow your truck." She glanced at Brody. "He's kind of big."

"How about we get this marriage thing done and

separate these two?"

"Okay, but afterward can I borrow your truck?"

"To hide the body?"

Becky half smiled. "I was thinking I'd go pick up some stuff for Sophie from the trailer. Ava said she'd help me get her crib, swing, and a few things. We both need more of our clothes."

No way in hell was he letting her go to that trailer without him. She'd run because she was afraid of Dylan. Becky's safety was Logan's responsibility. "We'll go by on the way home."

She rolled her eyes. "Don't trust me with your truck?"

Logan leaned close to her face. "Your protection is my responsibility. That's part of the deal. Plus, as a bonus, you get all my incredible manpower to do the heavy lifting."

Her breath hitched, and those tiny green flecks surfaced in her soft brown eyes. "And what do you get?"

"You. For a few months you're all mine." It should freak him out, but it didn't. He enjoyed dinners and midnight snacks with her. Liked her doing things in his house. And he'd like it even more if she were in his bed. But that was her decision.

Becky held up the contract. "Is that in here? That sex is part of the deal?"

Logan opened his mouth, but Brody spoke first.

"He wouldn't let me put that in."

"Shut up, Brody." Logan damn near punched his friend. Turning his back on the lawyer, he caught Becky's arm and guided her to the other side of the courtroom. Once out of hearing distance, he laid his hands on her shoulders. "Any decision about sex is between us." He wouldn't forget that look on her face after she'd almost lost control his arms. She'd been so gorgeous until that haunted look shattered her and made him feel like a total ass wipe. "I want you, but no one, and no contract, is going to compel you to have sex with me. It has to be what we both want with no regrets." He had enough of those, and so did she.

She tilted her head up, her eyes searching his. "I don't know how to do this."

"The temporary marriage?"

Becky pulled her mouth tight, seeming uncertain.

She looked too alone standing there and he didn't like it. "I'm a damn good friend, sweetheart. You can trust me."

Resolve settled in her gaze. "I can deal with possibly getting my heart bruised in this deal, but I can't lose Sophie. Please don't go out and pick up someone else. If you're seen, it could destroy my chances to keep custody of Sophie."

His chest hollowed. Her huge brown eyes were filled with vulnerability that unearthed his deepest protective instincts. He wanted her to trust him, but he hadn't earned it. He could clearly see that now. As it was, once she'd agreed to this scheme, he'd pulled some strings to get his marriage expedited without the required three-day waiting period. And now she was willing to give him her body to keep him from screwing around and hurting her chances to keep her baby.

Unable to stand it, he pulled her into his arms. The contract in her fingers scrunched between them. Threading a hand into her silky hair, he tilted her head back. "I won't do that, Bec. This deal is as important to me as it is to you and I won't jeopardize it. I don't cheat on my friends. While we're married, neither of us will step out."

She nodded. "Okay, let's do this."

"Finish reading the contract over, we'll sign, and get ourselves hitched."

• • •

Becky rubbed her neck and scanned the room she shared with Sophie in the trailer. It looked empty. In no time, Logan and Brody had loaded the crib, changing table, dresser, and swing into the truck.

She was really doing this, moving into Logan's home. As his wife. How was this going to work? "What if Logan's family hates me?"

"Screw them." Ava backed out of the closet with the last of the clothes and shoes.

"They're not going to think I'm good enough." She didn't think she was good enough.

Dumping the armload on the bed, Ava glared at her. "Why do you care what his family thinks if Logan doesn't?"

"He's doing so much for me, I want to do my part."

"Tell you what, we'll go shopping. New clothes will make you feel better."

Becky shook her head. "I got a few things after Sophie was born, I'm good."

Ava sighed. "The contract says Logan's going to provide for your expenses, and that covers clothes."

"Stop that. I'm not spending his money." She stuffed the last of the items into the big plastic trash bags. It wasn't fancy, but it'd get the job of moving her done. Being here in the trailer made her throat ache with grief for her mom. It was too quiet, too…empty. And soon it would sell. She had to do something about her mom's personal things in the next few weeks.

"Hey, you okay?" Ava tied up one of the bags.

"Yeah." She didn't want to talk about her mom right now, not with Logan around to see her if she got emotional. "Can't believe I'm married."

Ava wrinkled her nose. "That was the coldest excuse for a wedding I've ever seen."

"What did you expect?" She faced her friend. "It wasn't a real wedding, and when did you get all warm and romantic anyway?" Ava had told her to keep her heart out of it.

"He barely kissed you. You sure he knows what he's doing?"

Her stomach warmed at the memory. When the judge had told Logan he could kiss the bride, he'd taken both her hands in his warm steady ones, his eyes captivating her. Becky's nerves had tangled with that sweet rush of desire. That's what worried her, she'd never reacted to another man like she did Logan—what if he kissed her and she clung to him like a sex-starved monkey? Then he'd leaned in and bushed his mouth over hers. Tender, chaste, and sexy in its own way because he'd done just as he'd promised.

"He did that for me." That small gesture meant so much to her. She could trust him to care about her feelings. Logan wasn't a spoiled boy like Dylan, needing to grope Becky in front of his friends to prove he was a man. Logan was a man, a good man who she was coming to respect and trust more each day.

She scooped up the two bags of clothes and shoes, turned, and her stomach dropped out. "Logan." Damn it, how did he move so quietly?

He strode in and took the bags from her hand. "This all of it?"

Her skin tingled where his hand had brushed hers, but she couldn't read his gaze. "I think so." Could he tell she'd been talking and daydreaming about him? She had to get a grip—being here in her mom's trailer brought her emotions too close to the surface. "I just have a couple more things to do. Ava can drop me and Sophie off if you want to go."

"We already had this discussion, sugar. I'm not leaving you here alone. Not for a second. Take all the time you need." He headed out.

Becky turned on her friend. "You saw him standing there, didn't you?"

She shrugged. "He's kind of hard to miss. Big and sporting all that cowboy brawn." Ava frowned. "Although he barely looked at me on account of being too busy staring at you."

Becky ground her molars, hearing her words *he did that for me* like some lovesick teenager. "I should kill you. That lawyer would get me off. Brody doesn't like you."

Ava turned to talk to Sophie while fixing the baby's headband. "After most weddings there's a celebration. Or at least the groom takes the bride and her awesome attendants—that would be me—to dinner. If he's cheap, then a nice lunch. Hell, I'd even settle for pizza and beer. But no...we're doing manual labor moving his wife on her wedding day so your rich step-daddy doesn't have to pay for movers."

Sophie babbled, clearing enjoying her godmother's performance.

Ava nodded. "Exactly right, my little genius. Don't ever settle for a cowboy who marries you then expects you to cook dinner that same night. You deserve a man who wants to treat you right."

Becky rolled her eyes at her friend's preposterousness and turned.

Logan stared back from the doorway, his full mouth set in a grim line.

Oh come on. How many times was he going to sneak up on her while Ava was mouthing off? Planting a hand on her hip, she glared at him. "You can't just walk around without making noise. It's not polite."

"Want me to take lessons on being polite from your wedding planner over there?" Logan angled his head toward Ava but kept his eyes on Becky.

"You two need a wedding planner. Or at least a fake marriage planner." Ava tucked Sophie into her car seat and stomped to the door.

Logan stepped aside and sent her a challenging look. "Why's that?"

Ava rolled her eyes. "You need wedding rings to make this marriage look real." After dropping that bombshell, she left.

The silence in the room echoed. Desperate to fill the gap, she said, "I'm all finished. Let's go." She headed to the door.

Logan caught her arm, his eyes doing that intense spotlight thing on her. "You knew this wasn't going to be like a real wedding, right?"

"Stop." She firmed her spine. "I knew and so did Ava. She was running her mouth trying to keep me distracted."

"From?" His brow furrowed.

She took a breath.

"Oh. Christ, Becky, I didn't think. Your mom." He put

his hand on her face. "It's only been weeks since you lost her."

"Don't. Please." It came out a thick whisper.

He nodded, dropping his hand. "Okay. Let's go home."

Becky lost track of him for a few minutes while she got Sophie settled in the backseat of his truck and said good-bye to Ava.

Logan strode up to her. "I locked up." He gave her the keys, then helped her into the passenger seat.

Suddenly it was just the two of them and Sophie gurgling in the back. The truck shrank as Logan filled up the opened doorway.

Why didn't he move?

"Here." He held out something.

Becky took it and her breath caught on a shaft of grief and fierce tenderness. It was a picture of Becky's mom in a chair holding Sophie. Her nose clogged and her eyes burned.

Don't cry, don't.

"It was tucked into the mirror in your bedroom. She looks like you so it must be your mom." Logan gently brushed away a tear. "We'll get a frame so you can have her with you and Sophie in your new home. We're not leaving your mom behind, sugar."

His green eyes were filled with compassion. How did he so easily understand? But one glance at the tat on his biceps gave her the answer. He hadn't left his friends that died behind either, he carried them with him in that beautiful tribute. "Thank you."

He smiled, then closed her door.

Becky stared at her mom's image and whispered, "How do I not fall for him?"

Chapter Six

Logan looked up from chopping vegetables and damn near cut off his finger. Becky wore a striped casual dress held up by elastic that cupped her full breasts and flowed down to skim the tops of her bare feet as she walked toward him. The loose dress swayed around her long, curvy body and made him forget to breathe. For the first time today, she looked relaxed and so damn pretty.

"Logan!" Becky rushed in and grabbed the towel off his shoulder. "You're bleeding." She wrapped his cut finger in the towel.

Her scent wafted up from her freshly washed hair as she bent to check his finger. Honeysuckle, a sweet aroma that made his mouth water.

Becky lifted her head. "It's not too bad. You don't need stitches."

She was in total girl-next-door mode with her hair drying around her makeup free face. Wait, she said something, right? "What?"

"The cut on your finger." She lifted his wrist to display his towel-wrapped index finger.

Oh right, he'd felt a prick on his finger. But he was much more interested in Becky. "I'm making you dinner." Her friend's comments about the way Logan handled the ceremony today really bugged him. The marriage wasn't real, but they were going to be living together for three months. He hoped Becky would want to be in his bed—he could at least treat her as he would any lover. Take her out if they could get a sitter, buy her things, be considerate.

"That's nice, but I'm not big on blood in my salad."

"Picky."

"Get used to it. I like the toilet seat down, too. Where are your Band-Aids?"

"First aid kit in the drawer by the fridge." He followed her movements as she fished out the plastic kit. "I like your dress." Especially the way it shimmied around her sweet ass, hinting at her curves there. Curves he'd had in his hands when he'd kissed her.

Becky dragged him to the sink for the wash-and-disinfect routine. "I made a couple of them after Sophie was born. It covered the pregnancy fat and it's easy to breastfeed in."

His gaze dipped to the material stretched across her breasts. His mouth dried. It'd be so easy to slide the dress down... Lust fisted low in his belly and heat prickled his skin. The urge to pull her to him and take her mouth buzzed through him.

"There, all bandaged."

He blinked, trying to clear the haze of need rushing through him. "Thanks." He forced his gaze to his finger so he'd quit staring at her. "Nice job."

"I was studying to be a nurse." She returned the first aid kit to the drawer. "I volunteered in a VA hospital in high school and college." Adding the chopped vegetables to the salads, she looked back over her bare shoulder. "I'm hoping to go back to school after our deal is over."

Interest in her plans calmed his lust. "Hang on a sec while I get the steaks off the grill." Once he returned from the back deck, he plated the two steaks and added a microwave potato to each. He and Becky settled in at the table and he asked, "How long do you have left to finish your degree?"

She scooped out some butter to fix her potato. "About a year. I'll work too, and I'll have to find good childcare. But if I can do it, then I'll have a job that will let me take care of Sophie the way she deserves."

He liked that she was thinking ahead. "Quit your job now and look into going back to college. Find out when the new semester starts and start going as soon as possible. I'll cover the cost."

"I've thought about it and I don't think I should quit work." She shook her head. "You're going to help me with the lawyer fees and the settlement, that's all I want."

"Bec, we agreed that I'm covering your expenses." She needed to get over her resistance to him handling her bills. He leaned closer. "You can't work for Luce while married to me. No one would believe you're married to a man who can easily support you yet you continue to work nights and take your baby with you."

She cut into her steak and Logan set about eating his dinner, giving her space to think. The last couple nights, he and Becky had dinner together and discussed their marriage plan, and the story they'd tell about how they met. He was going to break the news to his dad alone. He didn't want Becky in the line of fire if the old man unleashed his disparaging, old-school bullshit attitude.

To Brian Knight, Becky wouldn't be good enough for his son.

To Logan, she was too good. Smart, sweet, and hardworking. Still grieving for her mother too, and he needed to keep her shielded. He'd make it brutally clear to his father that his wife would be treated with respect.

"You have a point that it could look suspicious if I kept a job like office cleaning at nights when I could be home with Sophie. I'll turn in my notice soon, but I'll keep sewing pageant dresses and make some money that way." Becky drank some of the milk he'd poured her. "Then I'll use the time to investigate colleges so I can return to school after our deal is over."

He could almost feel her holding herself back from his offer but he'd wear her down. "How long have you wanted to be a nurse?"

She took a breath. "It's been my dream since I was little."

He wanted to help her with achieving it. "Getting pregnant derailed that for you."

Her eyes slid to his. "That's not Sophie's fault. I love her more than anything. Whether or not I become a nurse, being her mom is the best thing I could ever have."

"I believe you. But I know what it's like to have a dream. I went after mine by going into the Marines. And this marriage is helping me attain another dream."

Becky tilted her head. "Camp Warrior Recovery. Tell me more about it."

It meant a lot to him that she remembered and understood what it meant to him. "I'm working with a psychiatrist, Dr. Wayne Malone, who specializes in combat post-traumatic stress disorder. We want to create a low-stress environment for veterans with PTSD who are having a difficult time assimilating back into civilian society. They can come here with other vets who are going through the same thing. They'll be able to fish, ride horses, walk the trails, and do some intensive therapy to learn coping strategies. It'll only be a small group at a time. We're starting with ten cabins." Logan fidgeted with his knife beneath her intense stare. His father considered therapy a sign of weakness. A minute ago he'd have said he didn't care what Becky thought.

But he did. His leg started to bounce beneath the table as the silence dragged out.

"How long have you been working on this?"

"Almost a year. Most people who see combat come home with scars. Everyone deals with it differently. Adam started Once a Marine, providing jobs for former Marines. Having that focus helped him cope." Reconnecting with his former lover, Megan, helped him even more, but that had nothing to do with this conversation.

"And you want to do this camp that will give vets with PTSD a chance to acquire the tools to cope without the pressures of civilian life distracting them."

Heat crawled up the back of his neck. Did that make him a total pussy? Recognizing that he'd let his father's voice in his head, he ignored it. "That's exactly what I want to do."

"I'm impressed. Can I help? If I'm not going to be working, I'll have time." Her eyes glowed in the fading sunlight. "Have you thought about adding some low-key music therapy? We had a pilot program at the VA hospital I volunteered at, and it seemed to help the vets as they were recovering from injuries and dealing with PTSD. Particularly the sense of isolation and inability to express their emotions. Or sometimes, it just eased them." She tilted her head. "For this camp, I'd think you could provide access to a few instruments, maybe give all the guests notebooks in case they want to write some songs as a way of expressing themselves."

Logan had heard of music therapy, but he was more entranced by Becky's passion. Covering her hand with his, he said, "I grew up around music, and yet, that hadn't even occurred to me. It's a good idea."

Becky flushed, her eyes lighting up. "If there's anything else you want me to do, I'm here. I can handle paperwork, phone calls, or any other menial stuff from the house and take that off your shoulders."

"You'd do all that?"

"Sure, I want to feel useful, and your camp interests me." Flashing him a grin, she added, "That's what wives do, right?"

His mouth dried with longing. She was so generous, offering to help him with his goals. That wasn't in the contract, no her offer was from her heart. To him, Becky was clean, fresh, and good.

On the flip side, his soul was stained with too many memories and an epic failure that would haunt him to his grave. His PTSD and flashbacks had rendered him emotionally broken. He'd never subject a woman to a lifetime of that. And she had a child…just the thought of a child relying on him made his heart pound erratically and sweat pop out on his back.

He'd learned to cope with his PTSD—alone. He didn't want to expose Becky, or any woman, to what he was in the darkest hours. Hell, his own mother had given up the fight for him when he'd been a kid. Now? No woman would fight for him, not once they knew him. But he had Becky for these few months and he was going to cherish that gift. Trying to regain control of himself after her *that's what wives do* comment, he stroked her left hand. "I'm supposed to get you a wedding ring."

She shook her head. "I don't want you to do that. I'll use my mom's rings."

Covering her hand, he studied her eyes. "Is that really what you want? I don't mind buying you rings, and you can keep them." He liked the idea that she'd have something from him to keep. To look at and remember him.

"Yes. If a man ever gives me a wedding ring, I want it to be a true symbol of love, like my mom's rings were to her."

His fingers curled around hers, as if he could stop another man from sliding a ring on her finger…and owning her heart. The possessive streak pushed him to lean into her. "You win, but right now, you're *my* wife."

• • •

His possessive claim raised the hairs on her arms, sharpening her awareness. Becky couldn't drag her stare from Logan's light green eyes boring into her. Seeing her. Wanting her. His sheer intensity pulled her closer, a magnetic tug she couldn't resist.

A shiver of seductive heat filled her belly. Made her lips

crave the touch of his.

His mouth tilted into a wicked curve. "Careful, baby. If I kiss you now, it won't be that chaste little peck you got earlier today."

Was he warning her or enticing her? Only inches separated them. "What will it be?"

"Our kiss. The one we both crave. I'm going to take my time, learning all the secrets of my wife's mouth." He stroked his thumb over her wrist and hand, long sweeps that raised excitement-bumps on her arms.

Why didn't he just kiss her? What was he waiting for? His fingers skimmed over her sensitive skin up to the inside of her elbow. Her nipples pebbled. A spike of pleasure arrowed to her core. She pressed her thighs together.

"Do you know how hot that is?"

"What?" Could he see her reaction?

"You licked your lips." He leaned a fraction closer. "You want my taste, sugar."

He stripped her control away with mere words. What would his kiss do to her? Becky wasn't sure she could handle it and surged to her feet, desperate for a distraction. "I'll do the dishes." Scooping up any dish she could grab, she rushed to the kitchen to deposit them in the sink. She spun and almost crashed into Logan.

He leaned around her to set his dishes down. Her breasts brushed his chest and she inhaled sharply, jerking her gaze up to his face.

"Know why I cut my finger tonight?"

Her pulse throbbed in her ears. "Why?

He skated the back of his knuckles over her face. "Because you walked out looking incredible in that dress. So fresh and pretty, and so goddamned real I forgot to breathe or watch what I was doing."

His words and touch, and the blaze in his eyes made her shiver. Heat from his powerful body poured over her. She couldn't talk, couldn't think of anything to say.

"Becky." His voice came out raspy. "I want to kiss my wife."

She had a word now. "Yes."

He skated his thumb down her throat to the fluttering pulse. "Tonight is only for kissing." Leaning down, he added, "We have three months together. You're going to take all the time you need because you're worth waiting for to have in my bed."

Becky had no chance to reply as his full, warm mouth glided over her lips.

Logan groaned. She felt him grab onto the counter, locking her between his powerful biceps. Angling his head, he licked and coaxed until she opened, giving him access. He tasted of dinner and that richer, masculine flavor that was all his. He dived in, his tongue commanding as he explored her, filling her with his taste.

Becky dug her fingers into his sides, desperate to hold on. Growing bolder, she tangled her tongue with his, getting more aggressive with every thrust. A whimper of burning need clawed up her throat. Every part of her ached to feel more of him, all of him.

He pulled back, his gaze scorching. Leaning his forehead against hers, he growled out. "Damn, sugar. You're killing me."

Her skin pulled tight, and need burned in her throat, down her chest, torturing her nipples. But he held his body back from hers, denying her what she craved. "You're not touching me."

Keeping his hands anchored on the counter, he leaned in, kissing from her mouth to her ear. "I'm trying to keep my promise. Kissing. Only kissing. Not stripping that dress off you and… Jesus, Becky." He buried his face in her neck.

His spicy, leather scent filled every empty part of her. But when he lightly scraped his teeth over her tender skin, hot stabbing aches made her squirm with the need for touch. He lashed his warm tongue over the sting, and Becky sank her fingers into his hair, holding him to her, desperate to be enveloped in his arms, surrounded by the hot feel of Logan.

Unable to bear it, she pressed her body into his hard chest, silently begging him to hold her. The contact tortured the hard points of her nipples. Against her belly his erection pulsed, scorching her. He gently bit, licked, and sucked the sensitive spot at the curve of her neck, shooting whips of hot pleasure through her. Sending her too high, too fast with nothing to hold onto. Finally she said, "I want you to touch me. Please."

• • •

Becky's taste was addictive, destroying his will. It was taking everything he had to keep his hands anchored on the counter. This was for her. Only her. Didn't matter how badly he wanted her, how desperately he longed to slide that dress down to explore her full breasts. To touch and taste, fit his mouth over her swollen nipples and suck. The roof of his mouth itched with imagining what her nipples would feel and taste like.

Wait. Her words seeded into his brain. She'd asked him to touch her. Finally, it penetrated his mind that while he was struggling to hold back, Becky burrowed against him. Her arms wrapped around his waist, her head against his shoulder, her breasts pressed into his chest; she was touching him everywhere she could.

"You need to be touched and held, don't you, sweetheart?"

A flash of shame or regret contracted her pupils before she dropped her gaze.

He was going to kick his own ass. "Talk to me. Please."

She looked back at him. "It's been awhile since anyone but my friends or Sophie have touched me. I just…" Her gaze flickered, but she held his stare. "There's nothing like the feel of a man's arms around me."

He'd seen that waver; someone had made her feel bad for needing to be held. She'd been used and made to feel worthless. That shit stopped here and now. Tugging her close, he caged her in his arms, holding her flush to his body. "You feel damn good in my arms, darlin'." He lowered his head, wanting to taste her mouth again.

"Logan."

He hesitated, willing to stop if that's what she wanted.

"I'm not saying I want to have sex right now, but you should know that I'm on birth control. I had a shot at my six week checkup after Sophie was born."

"Good to know. When you're ready, I'll use a condom, too. We won't take chances. But right now, I'm just kissing my wife until she's ready for more." He skimmed his mouth over hers.

A sudden pounding on the door cut off his sentence. He

jerked to full alertness at the aggressive knocking. What the hell?

Jiggy came tearing out of the hallway, barking.

He released Becky. "Stay here." He strode to the door where Jigs stood at attention. His ruff raised along his back. The little dude didn't lack courage. "Sit."

Jiggy dropped his butt down, but kept his gaze fixed on the door, issuing low warning growls.

He opened the door and felt like growling himself. "Dad."

Brian Knight took one step then froze when Jiggy growled louder. His father's face wrinkled in confusion. "What's that?"

What was his dad doing here? It couldn't be a coincidence he showed up on the day he married Becky, but how would he have found out? "A dog. What are you doing here?" His father didn't stop by for chats or a beer. Ever.

Ignoring the dog, Brian puffed up his chest and stormed into the house. Logan could have blocked him, but that wouldn't achieve anything.

By the chair, Brian crossed his arms. "You got married today."

Man, they'd have killed for this kind of rapid intelligence when he'd been on active duty in the Marines. He shut the door. "Yes."

"To a Rebecca May Holmes."

"How'd you hear so fast?"

"I'm friends with the husband of the judge's secretary. When the judge asked her to file the marriage certificate, she called me." His face darkened. "You snuck off and married her without a word to anyone. What'd you do, knock her up?"

Logan stomped hard on his rising anger. "No. I'm fulfilling my end of the contract by marrying and living on the ranch. On my birthday, I will own my land once and for all."

The older man looked around the house. "I'd like to meet your bride. I'm assuming this is the same woman you've had stashed in the house?"

"Another time. Becky is—"

"Right here."

Logan's breath caught as Becky walked out of the kitchen. She glided to a stop between them and flashed her beauty queen smile at his father. "I'm Becky Holmes." She chuckled. "Whoops, make that Becky Knight. It's going to take some getting used to."

Logan's brain kicked into gear. He wrapped an arm around her shoulders and pulled her to his side. "It sounds right to me, sweetheart." He shifted to his father. "My dad stopped by to congratulate us."

"I heard, how lovely." She held out her hand. "It's nice to meet you, Mr. Knight."

His father had no choice but to take her hand. "How did you and my son meet?"

Taking her hand back, she answered, "Lucinda introduced us and we've been friends for a while. Then we began dating and here we are married."

"In a courtroom? Why not have a wedding? Are you going on a honeymoon?"

Logan opened his mouth to put a stop to this inquisition.

Becky pressed her fingers into his stomach, silencing him. "It didn't seem in good taste to have a big wedding,

Mr. Knight. My mother just passed a few weeks ago. And a honeymoon is too difficult to arrange as I have a three-month-old daughter. Her name is Sophie. She's asleep right now or I'd introduce you to her."

"This is your second marriage?"

"First marriage."

"Enough." Logan wouldn't allow his father to grill and embarrass her. "Becky doesn't owe you explanations."

Frustrated anger crackled around his father like snapping flames. His arms and shoulders bulged beneath the blue chambray shirt. "You married a janitor who has a baby with some other man."

Adrenaline burned through his muscles. Taking his arm from Becky, he yanked open the door. "This is Becky's home. You aren't welcome here until you can treat her with respect."

His father barreled to the doorway, then looked him dead in the eye. "You can't even fulfill a man's bargain with honor." Then he strode off.

Logan shut the door and turned.

Becky wrapped her arms around herself. "This is going to be harder than I thought. He hates me."

Leave it to his father to ruin the moment. "It'll work out." It had to.

She shook her head. "What if he finds out?"

"Our marriage is legitimate, so there's nothing he can do."

Her eyes brimmed with worry. "But that contract, what if he discovers that?"

"He won't, but even if he did, I'll still have fulfilled the terms of my contract with him to get the land."

Becky rocked on her feet, worry spreading over her face. "I could lose Sophie." She trembled, holding her arms around her stomach. "What if I've made things worse, not better?"

"Becky, stop. It's going to be okay." He went to her, and stroked a lock of her silky hair. "It's been a long day, you're dead tired, and imagining the worst."

"You think so?"

She looked up at him like he had all the answers. Like he could save her and her child. She was so naïve and trusting. His past failure splashed across his mind and sweat popped out on his back. Sick memories played—a horror movie with no sound. Just the silence of death. Horrible underserved deaths. Logan's team was supposed to save them.

Supposed to.

But he'd failed and all those young girls died.

Jesus. Logan was no one's hero. The walls started closing in on him. Jerking around, he strode to the front door. "I need some air." He needed to get away, be outside, be alone, and pull his shit together.

Chapter Seven

A wet nose woke her up. "Jiggy." It was dark and cold, but she didn't hear Sophie stirring or crying. Pushing up on her arm, she looked in the crib. Her baby was sound asleep with her mouth opened, little chest rising and falling in her thick sleeper. Glancing at the clock, it was close to two a.m. Sophie usually slept through the night now, at least until five or six.

She lifted the covers, hoping Jiggy was just cold rather than needing to go outside. "Come sleep with me." He liked to curl up behind her knees.

He shoved his nose in her neck.

"Fine." She didn't want him getting desperate and peeing in Logan's house. Getting out of bed, she grabbed the extra blanket, wrapped herself in it, and half stumbled out to the living room. Jiggy shot out the front door, while Becky leaned against the doorjamb. Her feet were freezing.

"Go inside, Becky."

Becky yelped. "Logan?" Stepping out onto the porch,

she couldn't see anything. It was pitch black. The moon must be behind some clouds.

"Over here."

She turned in the general direction of the chairs. "What are you doing out here?"

"Can't sleep. Go back to bed. I'll watch the dog."

His voice didn't sound right. Too empty.

Not your problem, go back to bed.

"Aren't you cold?" She tried to see him and could barely make out his shape slumped in a chair.

"No."

"Why don't you watch TV? Or read?" Why sit here in the dark?

He sighed. "Can't be inside."

The utter emptiness in his voice worried her. Pulled her closer. She reached out and skimmed soft cotton. "Why?"

A hand clamped around her wrist. "Don't."

Her heart shot up to the throat. "Logan, what's wrong?"

"You can't help. You were right the first time you ran from me after I kissed you. Run now." He ripped his hand away. "Go."

Tremors that had nothing to do with the cold started from the center of her chest and radiated out until her teeth chattered. "Jiggy, come." Turning she rushed through the door, then stopped.

It was too cold outside.

Becky doubled back out to the porch. "Don't growl at me," she said softly. "I'm just giving you this." She slipped the blanket off her shoulders and draped it over him. Then she went inside, quietly closing the door.

Once back in her bedroom, she wondered what the hell

happened. That was not the man she knew. He'd been cold, distant…

Told her to run.

Jiggy whimpered at her bedroom door. He wanted to go back to Logan. Instead, Becky picked up the dog and put him in bed with her. Logan didn't want them.

Sometimes if felt as if no one wanted her.

• • •

"That wasn't so bad, was it, baby girl? Just a little cheek swab." Becky held her daughter close as she left the medical building, trying to quell her queasiness. The test to establish paternity had been simple and quick.

It was the repercussions that had her trembling. The results would be issued to the court, then her and Dylan's lawyers would get a copy and they'd go from there.

Becky kissed the soft fuzz coming in on Sophie's head. "I'm sorry, baby. You deserve a better father." She would be a good mother though. She had to.

Her stomach bubbled uneasily. She had to ask Logan for the lawyer's retainer. God, it made her sick to do it, but her lawyer had to have it. She'd stopped by the bank this morning to check on her loan—she'd been turned down. There were no other options.

Shifting Sophie, she unlocked the car and buckled Sophie into her car seat. Becky forced a smile for her baby then closed the door. Opening her side, she glanced at the truck driving down the aisle slowly.

Oh God. Her hand slid off the door latch. Dylan. He stopped, his big truck blocking her little car in the space.

The window rolled down. Fear and memories tangled. The way he'd grabbed the phone from her when she'd called 911. Hitting her. That punch in her stomach. She forced herself to get control and calm down. "What are you doing here?" His mirrored sunglasses prevented her from seeing his eyes.

He leaned his arm on the door. "Word is you've moved out of your trailer. People saw you loading up some guy's truck and you're living with him. That'll go over real good with the judge. You just don't know how to be anything but trash, do you?"

His taunt hit home, igniting her fury. "I'm not living with him, we're married."

Dylan fisted his hand, the muscles in his forearm bunching. "Who'd marry you?"

She lifted her chin, so tired of feeling powerless. "Logan Knight." That felt good, really good. Logan was a million times the man Dylan was, and Becky was proud to call him her husband. He treated Becky like she was valuable for more than sex.

Dylan yanked off his sunglasses, staring at her for long seconds.

Her pride withered under the weight of growing fear. Dang, maybe she shouldn't have provoked him. She glanced at Sophie in the backseat. Okay, she could grab her baby and run back into the medical building. They'd be safe—

"Bullshit." Dylan snapped. "You're lying. If you were married to a Knight, you wouldn't be driving that piece of shit." He ran his gaze down to her where she was twisting her hands. "I don't see a ring on your finger. No Knight would have you as more than a quickie or side piece." He laughed as he replaced his sunglasses then drove off.

With adrenaline whipping through her, Becky hurried into her car and left. Gripping the steering wheel, she glanced at her bare ring finger—her fault, she hadn't put her mother's rings on this morning. She wouldn't repeat that mistake. But right now, she kept watch on the rear view mirror as she drove the streets. She saw a lot of trucks, but none of them were Dylan's black Silverado 2500 turbo diesel—an exact model of the one he'd hit that poor man in, except he'd changed the color.

A noise penetrated her thoughts. What was that thumping? The whole car was jerking. More adrenaline released and her heart raced. The car bumped with a sickeningly familiar rhythm.

Flat tire.

Her head started to pound as she pulled off to the side and turned on her emergency blinkers. Sophie began to fuss. "Hang on, sweetheart." She got out of the car and circled it. The right rear tire was flat.

What if Dylan sabotaged her tire? There weren't that many cars on this two-lane road. He could come by and grab Sophie. Okay, that would be stupid, wouldn't it? But Dylan was used to getting his way. He was capable of anything.

The ache in her head intensified. Becky got in the car, fished out her phone, and called her best friend. It rang and rang. Glancing at her watch, she swore. It was just after two in the afternoon; Ava was in her dance class. Okay. Who else? Logan was her first thought. He had a way of calming her and making her feel safe, but she'd never asked for his cell number.

Sophie's fusses deteriorated into crying. Desperate, she tried another number.

"Becky?" Lucinda answered. "Oh, I heard the news. Thanks for inviting me to the wedding."

A car passed by, making her jump. Worry tightened her neck. "It wasn't really a wedding. Just a quickie ceremony. But I called because—"

"You're turning in your notice, right?"

Jerking her head around, she stared as a dark colored truck passed by. Relief sagged her shoulders. Not Dylan. "No, I mean I will have to, but I have a flat tire. Sophie's crying, I can't get a hold of Ava."

"Why didn't you call Logan?"

Another wail from her daughter made Becky wince. She reached back, rubbing her arm. "It's okay, Sophie." To Lucinda, she said, "Uh, I don't have his number." And yeah, didn't she feel stupid about that. "I'm kind of scared. Dylan was at the medical clinic." She quickly spilled out the encounter and described exactly where she was.

"Hold on, Becky."

The phone muted.

Her poor baby was getting more and more upset. Should she take her out of the seat? Would that be safe?

"Okay, hang tight. Logan's on his way."

"Logan?" Hot tears of relief burned her eyes. He was coming; they'd be okay. Becky blinked back the moisture.

"Yes, I called him. Why the hell didn't you have his cell number?"

"I don't know, it hasn't come up."

"He didn't know you were gone from the house. You two should communicate a little."

Her baby's screams nearly drowned out her boss's words. "Hang on." Putting the phone down, she got out of the car and rescued her daughter from the car seat. Once she retrieved the phone, she walked off the road, where it was safer. "I'm back."

"I'm glad you and Logan married."

Overwhelmed and unsure of what she was doing, she asked, "Did you plan this? I mean if Logan wanted a temporary wife, I'm sure he could find one easily, so why me?"

"I'd been thinking about it, and considering how to bring it up to you two when you called in a panic because Dylan was out of prison. Logan needed a wife. You needed help even before Dylan came back into the picture."

A truck approached and she tensed until she caught sight of Logan's dark hair in the driver's seat. "Logan's pulling up right now."

"Okay. We'll talk soon. And, Becky, I accept your resignation. I'll send you your last check."

"But what about next week? I don't want to leave you in a bind."

"I've got it covered. You just take care of that baby and my cousin." She hung up.

Logan strode across the debris to her car.

Huge and oh-so-capable, her cowboy was the best thing Becky had ever seen. Hurrying over to him, she said, "Thank you for coming. I wasn't sure what to do, and when Lucinda said you were on your way, I was so relieved."

He touched her face. "Hey, it's okay. We're going to take care of this, then we'll get you and Sophie home safe."

Home safe. Once she'd craved a home, but right now, his touch felt like home and safety in one package. He'd come for her and that meant more than she could adequately express. For the first time in a long time, Becky didn't feel alone. Pulling herself together, she nodded and stepped back. "It's the right rear tire."

He peered down to the left side of the car. "Then you got a bigger problem."

Frowning she followed his gaze and saw that her left side was flat, too. "Shit."

. . .

It took Logan less than two minutes to find where the tires had been punctured with something sharp. Her tires had been in bad shape to begin with, so it hadn't taken much. He should never have let her drive on these.

When he rose to his full height, the baby was screaming and Becky was frantically trying to calm her. Like history repeating itself from that first night he'd found them hiding in his bedroom. Except this time, the baby didn't trigger his PTSD; instead, she and Becky roused his fiercely protective instincts. Maybe he couldn't hold and play with the baby, but he wanted her safe, fed, and content, not stranded, frightened, and hungry. After all, it wasn't Sophie's fault that he was haunted by his failure that resulted in the murder of an innocent baby and school girls. "She's hungry?"

Becky looked around, her dark eyes enormous in her pale face. "Yes."

He wrapped his arm around her, feeling the strain in her muscles. She'd been scared, alone, and stranded with a baby. Containing his fury at himself for not making sure she had his number in her cell, he guided her to his truck and opened the passenger door. "Sit in here and you can feed her while I call a tow truck." He helped her up to the seat, then unbuttoned his shirt and slipped it off, leaving him in his white T-shirt. "Use this to cover up."

She took the shirt, her fingers brushing his. "Thank you."

"It's going to be fine." He took out his phone and made the call. A few minutes later he got into the truck. "Tow truck will be here in twenty. You okay if we wait?"

She nodded, but chewed on her bottom lip. "After paying for the paternity test today, I only have about four hundred dollars in my account. Will that cover towing and the two tires? Uh, I also need to get more diapers and dog food for Jiggy."

He didn't say anything for a minute. The baby's contented sucking sounds filled the cab. His skin grew tight realizing how damned vulnerable Becky and the baby had been today. And he hadn't even known she was gone. That was square on him for pulling back like he had. Because after that confrontation with his dad, then seeing Becky so worried and looking as if he could keep her and Sophie safe, the claustrophobia and nightmares had started again. So he did what he always did—withdrew to control his emotions and get level.

Why the hell would Becky have told him a damn thing? He'd cut her out emotionally. And now here she was chewing her lip trying to figure out how to pay for tires. "It's more than enough since you're not paying for it." He turned to look at her. Even pale and tired, she was damned beautiful sitting there with his shirt thrown over her, feeding her baby.

She switched Sophie to her other breast. Logan should look away, but the tenderness of seeing Becky take care of the baby eased the rage that had been boiling in him since the encounter with his father. Once she settled his shirt over her again, she lifted her eyes to his.

"I talked to my lawyer. She needs the retainer Monday. If you can do that, I'll take care of my car."

Logan glanced at his watch. It was after three on Friday afternoon. He'd made Becky promises and hadn't followed through. She'd done her part, playing his wife when his dad had shown up the night they married. But he hadn't done his, instead she felt alone and unable to ask him for what she needed. He had to fix this. "I've got your car covered. We'll stop by the lawyer's office on the way home and I'll take care of the retainer."

"Thanks." She rubbed her forehead. "I'm sorry to ask."

Without thinking, he reached over, taking her hand. "Headache?"

"Long day."

"And you hate taking money from me." Or food until she'd decided she earned it by working in his house. "Why?" He wanted to understand. Now that he was with her again, letting his guard down, he was unable to resist wanting to know everything.

She leaned back, closing her eyes. "It's like getting the free lunches at school. It felt like everyone stared. Kids made fun of me, well of all of us, in the program. And those lunch ladies, always asking if my mom was doing any better and telling me to take good care of her. I didn't know what I was supposed to do."

Logan tightened his hand around hers. "About what? You were a kid. You couldn't exactly work." He regretted now not doing a deeper background. He'd checked the one they had on file, and he'd googled Dylan Ridgemont and the hit-and-run.

"My mom's grief. I couldn't bring them back. I was trying to be good, but I was having nightmares about the fire and was afraid to sleep alone."

Oh hell, he'd definitely missed something. "Becky, look at me."

She turned her head, her eyes shadowed.

He touched her face, wanting to ease the strain there. "Sweetheart, what fire?"

"A house fire. I was six. When my mom and I came home, our house was engulfed. Huge flames coming out the windows."

Shit. "Who was home that day?"

"My father and brother. Tyler was nine. They couldn't get to them. There was nothing they could do except hold my mom back."

Jesus. She'd only been six. Her world had been destroyed. Logan had thought he had had a bad time of it? His mom was alive. Maybe he hadn't seen her much, but the possibility was always there. "I'm sorry." Those words were so damned inadequate.

She sat up, shifting Sophie and adjusting her clothes. "It got better. Before the fire, my mom had a part-time business sewing pageant dresses. When she recovered a little, she turned it into a full-time business and things were fine."

This explained why Becky had a maturity and emotional depth most twenty-two-year-olds, like his younger sister Pam, hadn't yet attained—she'd lived through some tough times at a very young age. He kept touching her face. "It sucked, baby. For you and your mom."

"I was young, but my mom, she lost so much that day. It

took her a while just to function again."

Logan could see the old pain in her eyes. Her need to be touched and held went deeper than an asshole ex. "You suffered too. That's not your mom's fault, I'm sure she did the best she could. Did you try to take care of your mom?"

Her eyes widened. "I didn't know how. That's one of the reasons I want to become a nurse. They know how to take care of people."

She took his breath away with comments like that. She'd felt powerless as a child, and instead of crying about it, she figured out a way to get the power she needed as an adult. Becky had a tender heart, but she was strong, resilient, and kickass in her own way. If money was her only obstacle to her nursing degree, he was going to fix that and make it happen for her. That was something tangible and real that he could give her.

Chapter Eight

Becky eyed her hand-drawn design. Her latest client, Marla, had darker skin, and that would make the pale yellow color look like a strip of morning sunlight across her body. The diagonal, off-one-shoulder cut added to that imagery, plus it was very sensual. But it needed a tad more oomph. She pondered that while methodically sewing the pieces of the dress together on her portable sewing machine.

The doorbell rang.

Jiggy raced out to bark at the door in case Becky didn't understand the concept of the doorbell. She set the dress aside and followed her dog to discover three women on the porch. "Hi Lucinda." Her former boss was dressed casually in jeans and a T-shirt, her dark hair loose and wavy around her shoulders. But the other two had her at a loss. "Uh, Logan's not here, he's out checking on some sick cattle, but I can call him if you need me to." She had his cell phone number now, and generally knew his schedule. He preferred to work the ranch in the morning and his camp in the afternoon. But his father kept making more and more demands on Logan's time.

Lucinda cut into her thoughts and held out an envelope. "I brought by your final paycheck." She nodded at the two women with her. "This is Pricilla, Logan's stepmother, and his sister. They insisted on accompanying me."

A woman with chic dark hair and the bluest eyes she'd ever seen held out her hand. "Hello, Becky. Congratulations on your marriage."

"Thank you." After shaking hands, Becky smoothed her tank top, and tried not to think about her worn jeans or bare feet. Oh Lord, her hair—she'd clipped it up to get it out of her way.

"This is my daughter, Pam."

The girl was around Becky's age. She had a heart-shaped face with blue-gray eyes, and she was rocking a short skirt and boots. Becky crossed one foot over the other, wishing she was better dressed. But at least she could show some manners. "Would you like to come in? I'm sorry for the mess, I wasn't expecting company." She glared at Lucinda.

Pricilla glided past her. "We're not company, we're family. No need to fret. We really need to get working on your reception."

"Reception?"

"Mom loves any excuse for a party." Pam bent down to Jiggy. "Oh, who's this? He's so sweet."

"Where would be the best place for us to work?" Pricilla looked around the living room and dining room covered in material.

Becky couldn't get her bearings. She focused on Pam

first. "His name is Jiggy." Her dog climbed up on Pam's lap. "He's a bit of a flirt with women."

"Maybe we could work out back on the deck?"

Becky turned to her mother-in-law. "I'm a little confused. Logan and I aren't having a reception."

Pricilla smiled and put her hand on Becky's shoulder. "I'd really love to do this for you. I want to show off Logan's bride and my new daughter-in-law to all of Dallas. It'll be lovely, you'll see." She walked to the table, efficiently cleared a spot, sat, and turned on her iPad. "We'll hold the reception here on the ranch. The side yard at our house will do nicely. I'll hire the caterers and—"

"Don't back down." Pam stood at her side, holding Jiggy.

Ah, an ally. She nodded her thanks and turned at attention. "Pricilla."

"Yes, dear?"

Becky judged her to be halfway into her forties, that place where beauty matures into a polished attractiveness, but she didn't see any malice in her eyes, just determination. After the tension with Logan's dad, the best thing she could do was get this woman on her side. Becky settled in a chair next to her. "Logan and I married quietly for a few reasons, not the least of which is my mother just passed away. I'm not comfortable having a reception." She let grief thicken her voice. "It would be disrespectful to her memory and, frankly, painful."

"Oh. I guess Brian did mention that." The other woman laid her hand over Becky's wrist. "I'm so sorry. How long has it been?"

There was true sympathy in her eyes. "Thank you. About six weeks. She had cancer."

"How sad. Maybe a big reception isn't the best way to go." Disappointment settled around her eyes and shoulders. "I really wanted to do this for Logan."

Lucinda sat across from Becky. "Aunt Pricilla, Logan doesn't care about parties. He'd just want you to accept Becky."

"But that's the point." She traced her finger around her iPad. "The marriage was so quick, we need a symbol to show that we support Logan."

This wasn't what Becky had expected. Logan's dad had come across as angry, controlling, and confrontational, while Pricilla chewed her lip in concern.

"You can't fix everything with a party." Pam dropped into the seat by Lucinda.

Pricilla closed her eyes, as if defeated by her daughter's words.

"Logan won't come. He never comes to any of your parties unless Dad bullies him."

"He would for his wife. A reception is out." Pricilla lifted her chin, regaining her poise. "I know, we'll do a low-key barbeque. Just introduce Becky to a few people, make it official. Of course Logan will come."

Becky was still reeling from the loaded subtext of the mother-daughter exchange. After meeting Brian, she wasn't sure what she expected, but this warm, sincere woman wasn't it.

Lucinda cut into her thoughts. "That would work. Small, intimate, it won't overwhelm Becky or make her uncomfortable given that her mom so recently passed."

Pricilla nodded. "Family and a few close friends." She turned to Becky. "How many people will you be inviting?

Let's keep it down to a hundred or so total."

"A hundred is small?" She had the sensation of getting caught up in a wave and being swept away—totally unable to see all the undercurrents snapping and popping beneath her.

"Fifty," Lucinda said. "Hamburgers and hot dogs. Cold salads." She shifted her gaze to Becky. "It's a good way to introduce you as Logan's wife and Sophie as his stepdaughter."

True. She was supposed to play her part, not make it harder on Logan. He apparently had enough issues with his family. "Okay. But absolutely no gifts."

Pricilla said, "Fifty to seventy-five. Gifts optional. How many people do you want to invite?"

Who would she invite? Wait. Damn, Pricilla was good. "No gifts. I'm not budging on this."

A frown marred the smooth skin of Pricilla's forehead.

Becky softened her tone. "It's just not the time for a party like that. Maybe we could do something on our first anniversary?"

"Oh, that'd give us a year to plan it!" Excitement shone in Pricilla's eyes. "Maybe you could renew your vows or something symbolic. Yes, that's what we'll do. This small barbecue to introduce you in a few weeks, between fifty and eighty guests, then next year, a huge event!"

Becky blinked at the way her mother-in-law kept massaging the number of guests. But her excitement was very real. "You like to throw a party."

Pam laughed. "Mom lives to entertain."

Pricilla flashed Becky a smile. "I'll teach you all the tricks. Brian is going to spend the next few years training

Logan in the management end of the ranch."

"And break Abby's heart. Hell, she's practically running the entire horse program now."

"Pam, there's more to running a horse and cattle ranch than just training the horses."

"You sound like Dad. Abby knows every inch of this ranch, every—" She clamped her jaw. "Forget it. No one listens."

Becky cut her gaze between the younger girl's angry eyes and her mother's admonishing ones. Fortunately, Jiggy nudged her leg just as Sophie began to cry. "Excuse me, that's my baby." She escaped to get Sophie, then returned a few minutes later.

Pam jumped up and raced around the table. "Hi there, what's your name?"

Becky was warming to Logan's sister. "Her name is Sophie. Would you like to hold her? She might fuss though, she's probably hungry."

"I'd love to." She held out her arms. Once she had Sophie in them, she returned to her seat, then laughed. "Jiggy, are you checking to make sure I'm taking care of your baby?"

Becky glanced over. Jiggy had his front paws on the chair.

"Sorry about that. He doesn't usually bother us at the table, but he's protective."

Pam stroked Jiggy's ears. "Every girl should have a protector."

For a second, Becky forgot the other three women sitting at the table. There was something so sad about Pam, a loneliness that shrouded her, keeping her separate. "Yes they should," she agreed. How was it possible that Becky felt a kinship with her when Pam came from wealth and she came from nothing? Yet she did. "What do you do, Pam? Are you in college?"

"I got kicked out for too much partying."

At the same time, Pricilla said, "She's taking a year off to compete in barrel racing."

Well, crap. Becky had stepped into another steaming pile of family tension. What did she say now?

Pricilla rose. "My turn to hold the baby." She glanced over at Becky. "Okay?"

"Sure."

Her mother-in-law's face softened as she lifted Sophie from Pam. "Well, look at you. Such pretty eyes."

Becky's chest hurt seeing the older woman with Sophie—a youngish grandmother. This was what she wanted for her daughter, but it wasn't real. After a few months, she and Sophie would be alone again.

Sophie's cries got her attention. Becky took her from Pricilla. "Thanks. Does anyone mind if I feed her here?"

Pricilla went back to the head of the table. "Of course not. Go right ahead."

Becky got Sophie settled just as the door opened behind her. She didn't have to turn around to know who it was. The electrical currents running up her back and lifting the fine hairs on her arms told her.

Logan.

Her skin almost sizzled when his shadow fell over her. His warm hand covered her shoulder. "Sugar."

With Sophie nursing, all she could do was tilt her head back. Logan looked down at her, his light eyes a startling contrast in his darker face. He lowered his head and brushed his mouth over hers. His lips were warm and firm and for that brief second, it was like being claimed. As if she belonged to Logan, mattered to him.

Then she remembered what he'd told her right before the marriage ceremony.

There will be times we need to touch, and probably kiss, to keep the image up.

Right. Okay, she could do this. "I didn't expect you home so soon."

He brushed his thumb along her cheek. "I thought you'd like that tour I promised you."

"Really? I'd love it. Can we see the horses? Can we go now?"

He grinned at her. "You look a little busy here."

She'd forgotten the three women in her house. Having Logan's attention hone in on her, offering to take her out to see what he'd been working on, scrambled her brains. "Right. Another time." She tried to smile as if it wasn't a big deal.

Pricilla rose, kissing her stepson's cheek. "Logan, congratulations on your marriage. We're planning a barbeque to introduce Becky."

Logan cast his gaze around the table. "Hi, Pam, Lucinda. Looks like you ambushed Becky while she was working."

Sitting down, Pricilla gave Becky her full attention. "Do you sew your own clothes?"

"Some of them. But this is a gown for a beauty pageant."

Pam leaned forward. "Are you in a pageant?"

"Not anymore. I did pageants before college. But this dress I'm working on is for another contestant."

Logan put his hand on her shoulder. "Becky won enough pageants to get a scholarship to college. She's going to return to finish her nursing degree soon."

The pride in his voice was all part of the image. Too bad the flutters in her chest didn't know that.

"Very nice," Pricilla glanced at her. "Now that you're married, you won't need to take on sewing work." She nodded toward Becky's hand. "Pretty wedding rings. Simple and classic. Did you pick them out?"

She could almost feel the other woman's caution. "We decided on these together." That was as close to the truth as she could get.

Pricilla's smile lost the cautious edge and morphed into a brilliance. "They're lovely."

Right then, Becky loved her new mother-in-law. Pricilla had a stunning wedding set with gleaming diamonds that was probably worth more money than Becky would see in a decade. Yet her compliment was genuine. She'd just wanted Becky to be happy with the rings. "Thank you."

Logan jumped in. "Time to end this meeting, ladies. I promised to show my wife around our land."

Pricilla closed up her iPad. "Fine, but no backing out on this barbeque."

Pam stayed seated. "Can I stay and babysit Sophie? She just ate so she should be fine. I'll call you if she cries or anything."

Having only met Pam today, Becky wasn't sure that was a good idea.

Lucinda stood. "Pam's great with kids, Becky. You can trust her."

"Please?"

Becky looked up at Logan. Pam was his sister, he would know.

He nodded, then said to his sister, "Give me your phone, I'll put Becky's cell in there."

In a flurry of activity, Lucinda and Pricilla left, Becky showed Pam around and familiarized her with Sophie's routine, and then she was in the truck with Logan.

Alone. Without Sophie as a buffer.

• • •

"Each cabin will have an efficiency kitchen."

Becky listened as Logan led her through rooms with framed walls.

"There will be a bedroom, bathroom, living area, and a front porch overlooking the pond."

She studied the space as they headed to the little porch. "It's peaceful here overlooking the water."

Logan moved behind her, his warmth a counterpoint to the cool breeze. "I came here all the time when I was a kid. It wasn't much then. A few years ago, I had the pond enlarged and restocked with fish. A couple guys and I built that deck for fishing."

She lifted her face to his. "Tell me more about your plans."

He took her hand and tugged her along beside him. "I can show you." He led her to a trailer. "This is a temporary office to work from and for the construction crew to use as needed." He led her up an aluminum ramp into a private office. Simple and functional with a built-in desk at one end and deep couch at the other. They went into a larger room, bypassed the conference table and side bar equipped with a coffeemaker, microwave, and small fridge, and stopped at blueprints spread out on a drafting table. On the wall over that were computer-generated renderings of the finished camp.

Entranced, she studied the pictures. The buildings were warm and rustic. The cabins formed a half circle around the pond, while the two larger structures were farther back.

Logan's body heat spread over her back as he pointed to the bigger structures in the pictures. "In that main building there will be a mess hall, rec area, and group therapy rooms. Dr. Malone and his staff will have their own offices for private therapy. There's also an indoor pool and spa, and a small gym, although we're encouraging outdoor activities for the more physically-able guests."

She wanted to hear every word, yet his nearness distracted her. "This is going to be amazing."

He glanced down at her. "I talked to Dr. Malone about your idea of adding in music. He strongly supports it, agreeing that keeping it a low-key option is best." He reached past her. "We've repurposed this space right off the rec room for it."

A wave of warmth filled her with a sense of being a part of something important. Logan had listened to her, valued what she had to say. Emotion climbed up her throat, embarrassing her. She took a breath and shifted her focus. "You mentioned fishing, hiking, and horseback riding, too."

He settled a hand on her waist. "I'm acquiring the horses now, working with them and hoping I can get Abby to help me."

It took her a second to place the name. "She's your other sister?"

"Yes." His jaw bulged for a second. "Abby's not like

Pammy. She's angry at me."

"Why?"

He looked down at her. The overhead lights bounced off his dark hair, emphasizing his strong bone structure. His sister Pam had a much more delicate build, brown hair, and lighter skin. He must have gotten his darker coloring and unique green eyes from his mother.

"I'm good with horses, but Abby is amazing. Like nothing I've ever seen. She knows horseflesh, and can spot a fast runner, a good cutter, even a horse who will do better with a child. She can get more out of a horse than any other person breathing."

"That makes her angry?"

"No. In Abby's mind, I'm the interloper that ruined everything in the family, including her chances of getting control of that ranch."

She tried to makes sense of it all. "But all you want is this piece of the ranch."

He nodded.

"Why isn't she mad at your father?"

"It's easier to blame me. When I first came to live here, Pricilla hadn't known about me. My father just showed up and announced that I was his son."

That was unbelievable. "He'd never told her?"

"No. She knew about his brief marriage to my mother, that was common knowledge. But few people knew she was pregnant when she ran off. When I came to live with them, it was an ugly time. Pricilla tried not to hate me, but I'm sure part of her did. And Abby was just old enough to pick up on that."

She couldn't imagine. "That had to be awful for you."

"Wasn't fun for Pricilla either. Believe me, I didn't make it easy on her. When she tried to be kind, I was a snarly little bastard."

"Did it ever get better?"

He smiled. "I don't know how Pricilla's lived with my father so long and not become a raving bitch, but she hasn't. We thawed over time, probably a lot of that was Pammy. She followed me around and I secretly liked it. Pricilla loves her daughters, and since Pammy loved me, we had to find a way to co-exist. After a year or two, I realized Pricilla wasn't all that bad and stopped working so hard to make her every waking moment miserable."

Becky leaned her head back against his shoulder. "Pricilla wanted to have a big reception." She told him the whole story.

"Luce had a point. It's a good idea for us to be seen as a couple. Not just for me, but for you and Sophie, too."

"True." Logan was keeping his word. Yesterday, once the tow truck had taken her car away, he'd driven them to the lawyer's office and paid the retainer. And today, her car had been delivered to the ranch with four new tires. "Thank you for the tires on my car."

He brushed his hand up her arm. "I want you and Sophie safe."

Damn, he was doing it again, creating the illusion that he cared. "No one can see or hear us, you don't have to say things like that. Or touch me."

He turned her in his arms, spreading his hand over her lower back. "Is that what you think?"

The masculine scent of soap, leather, and hard work clung to him and Becky wanted to inhale it so deep into her lungs she'd keep it forever. Combined with the feel of his hand wide and possessive on her back, she melted more with every passing second. Struggling to regain her bearings, she said, "It's what you told me. Like when you kissed me today in front of your family. That was for them." Right?

His eyes caught the sunlight streaming through a window, turning to green fire. He cupped her nape, sliding his thumb long the side of her throat. "It should have been."

Tingles fanned out from his touch. "It wasn't?"

"Sugar, you're doing something to me. When I got back to the house and saw the cars there, the burn of anxiety started in on me."

"Why did that bother you?" She wanted to understand Logan better. Most of the time, he seemed so calm and in control. But the night she'd found him sitting in the dark on the porch, the tension coming off him had been sharp and jagged.

"My house, this land, it's the place I come to be alone and beat back the PTSD when it rears up. Here I have complete control."

He was telling her something important and she wanted to make sure she grasped what it was. "What does that control mean to you?" She didn't know a great deal about PTSD, but she wanted to. Logan was building a compound here to help vets who were dealing with it and it mattered to her.

His hand on her back stiffened and his thumb on her jaw froze.

She gripped his waist, desperate to hold onto him and the moment. "You told me I can talk to you, that no one is judging us when it's just you and me. You can tell me."

He shook his head.

Before she could think, she blurted out, "I'll go first then. I'm afraid I'll never have what my parents had—real love. That no one will ever really want me for just me. They only want me to bang the beauty queen then leave."

As soon as the words were out, she regretted it. She'd just bared her soul to him. Aside from losing Sophie, that was the dread that Becky carried each and every day. That she just wasn't loveable for herself.

To a strong, powerful man like Logan, that had to sound pathetic. Would he dismiss her like most everyone else?

Chapter Nine

A bolder lodged in her chest as she waited to hear what Logan would say. How young and self-absorbed did it make her sound that here she was getting ready for a battle to keep Sophie safe from Dylan, and she told him her deepest fear was not being loved?

"I should go back and check on Sophie."

Logan's hand firmed on her back. "Pam will call if Sophie needs you."

She opened her mouth, desperate for another way to break this awful sick feeling.

Logan cut her off. "The beauty queen routine you showed me is hot. Sizzling hot."

That's when he'd first kissed her. Of course it was.

"But the way you are right now as the real Becky? That's the woman I want to have dinner and hang out with, then take to my bed to figure out all the ways I can make her come. That's the woman I'd want to wake up with and make love to as the morning light streams in." His chest expanded beneath his T-shirt, and the muscles beneath her fingers tensed. "You're the woman I want to try to talk to."

She couldn't move beneath the cascade of his words. He saw her as real and worthy. That held her captive. Becky waited, letting him work out what he could tell her.

Finally he took a breath. "I get claustrophobia, so bad that sometimes I can't go through a door into the house. And if there are people in there, it's worse."

The raw, living vulnerability in his eyes shook her right to her bones. Something beyond awful had happened to him. She thought back to the night she found him on the porch and he'd said he couldn't sleep.

"That's why you couldn't come in that night on the porch."

"Yes."

"Were you angry at me? Because we're in your house, causing you to have this reaction?" He'd been hurting and she'd just left him there.

He shifted his hand, sliding it beneath her tank, his warm skin marking her lower back. It was shockingly intimate and soothing at the same time. "When you touched me, it was all I could do not to pull you into my lap and hold you." He paused a beat. "But I knew that once I started touching you, I wouldn't have stopped."

"Even if I told you to?" She was getting drawn deeper and deeper into him, and every layer she peeled back fed her desperation to know, see, and feel more of him.

"Would you have?"

With his eyes commanding hers, his hands imprinting his touch on her back and nape, while his thumb stroked her skin, the answer was inevitable. "No." Just like when he'd kissed her the first time, and she'd wrapped herself around him. Yet her weakness and loss of control didn't appall him.

"That's why I sent you in the house that night. I knew if I started, you'd let me keep going even if you weren't ready. I'm not going to use you like that, but you came back and gave me that damn blanket."

She shivered beneath his gaze, too many thoughts and feelings crowding her mind; desire, heat, lust, and a deep need to keep this connection between them. "It was cold outside."

He smiled at her. "That right there? That sweet caring is what's shredding my control. I damn near begged you to let me hold you then, give you as much pleasure as you could take." His eyes burned into hers. "You asked why I kissed you today."

She hadn't exactly asked, but it didn't matter. "Why?"

"Because when I touch you, it all gets easier. Kissing you today was like that blanket—warm, soft, and giving me a little protection." He tilted in, his attention 100 percent on her. "I kissed you for me, but I stopped at a quick kiss for you."

Her breath caught and she leaned into the slow, easy strokes of his thumb. Craved it.

"I won't let our kissing and touching get out of control in front of other people. You can trust me for that."

The way he'd heard her and cared for her feelings ripped away her reservations and worries. Logan needed her. She stared at his mouth.

"But if I kiss you now, I'm not stopping." He skated his thumb over her bottom lip. "I'll start here. Then I will strip you naked, lay you on the couch in my office, and kiss my fill of you."

His eyes blazed with greedy fire as he drew his thumb down her throat, sliding over her tank to the side swell of her breast. Her nipples tingled.

"No matter how many times I make you come like that, it won't be enough, will it?" His cheekbones darkened to a dusky red. "You'll still ache to be filled." Logan tugged her hips to his.

The long thick column of his erection pressed against her belly. A deep emptiness throbbed between her thighs while her panties grew wet, her body too sensitive.

Logan wrapped his arm around her waist, lifting her eye-to-eye. "You're my girl who needs to be touched and held, and I'm going to hold you when I thrust into you, filling you as full as you can take, and look into your eyes as we both come undone together."

She shivered, nearly dizzy with need as she dug her fingers into the slab of muscle on his sides. "Logan."

He wrapped an arm around her back, his other pulling the clip out of her hair and combing his fingers through the tresses. Gentle patience touched his eyes, a brief calming of the flames burning in them. "We have a few months together. Don't rush this if you're not ready. If you want to wait, I'll take you to see the stables and meet my horses."

Her throat thickened with sensual trust she didn't ever recall experiencing before. She went up on her toes. "I don't want to stop."

Then she kissed him.

• • •

Logan shuddered as her words echoed in his brain. Half of him wanted to rip her clothes off and sheath his cock deep inside her, feel that essence that made her alive and vibrant. She had the power to shove back the ugliness inside of him, the memories and failures that shadowed his soul. But the other half of him wanted to savor Becky.

Don't rush her. She deserves better.

He secured his hand in the warm silk of her hair, tilted her head back, and devoured her mouth. She responded, tangling her tongue with his as if she was starved for him. Oh hell yeah, she wanted this as much as he did. Logan swung her up into his arms, carried her to his office, and kicked the door shut, sealing them in his private space. He set her on her feet.

Becky broke the kiss and stepped back.

He fought a suffocating wave of disappointment, that crushing sense of aloneness that had been growing in him. "Do you want to slow down? Stop?"

She shook her head, her honey locks sliding around her bare shoulders as she fished her cell from her pocket and set it on his desk. "I just want to make sure I hear the phone if Pam needs me." Becky reached behind her back beneath her shirt.

His heart pounded and anticipation simmered and popped. "What are you doing?"

She grasped her bra straps beneath the tank and tugged them down her arms. "My bra is functional, but not attractive. I'm getting it out of our way." She tossed the garment on the end of the couch.

The small room heated even though he'd flipped on the air conditioner. Beneath the white tank, he could see the outlines of her heavy breasts, the fat dark nipples poking against that white material. "More." The word came out a thick demand. Looking into her eyes, he swallowed once. "Show me how beautiful you are."

Her eyes darkened as she gripped the bottom of her tank and tugged it up slowly, baring the top of her loose jeans, followed by inch after inch of pale skin, and then her rib cage.

He fisted his hands, struggling to stand down. Not touch her, not yet.

She yanked off the shirt, her swollen breasts bouncing free. His mouth dried with a desperate need to taste her dark nipples. They stood rigid and begging to be licked and sucked. His resistance broke and he closed the distance, filling his palms with her breasts, gently thumbing those tight peaks.

Becky shivered.

Leaning in, he licked her lips, and kissed to her ear. "You want my mouth on your nipples, don't you?"

"God yes."

Her skin tasted so damn good, but it wasn't enough. Sucking on her collarbone, he lifted his head to let her pull his shirt off. Unable to wait, he dragged his tongue over her nipple.

Becky hissed the sweetest sound, telling him all he needed to know. Her fingers dove into his hair, tugging him closer to feel her heart pounding.

He leaned up to kiss her. "Your mouth tastes good. I want to see all of you. Will you let me?"

She nodded, her fingers sliding to unbutton her pants for him.

Her trust flooded him with the drive to make this good for her, to show her that she was special. Catching her hands, he guided her to sit on the couch, pulled off her boots and socks. Brushing her hands away, he dragged her pants off, leaving Becky in a scrap of black panties. Logan sat back on his heels. His cock throbbed and pulsed brutally against his zipper, but the sight of Becky on the black couch was so damned hot, he drank her in.

He palmed her calves, feeling the muscles there, then eased them apart. The silky material of her panties clung to her center. His heart pounded, his blood pumped. Heat bloomed over his face and chest. "I can see how wet you are."

Her hands clenched on the couch at her hips. "I—"

Slapping his hands down on the couch, he crowded in close to her. "Don't apologize for that."

There in her eyes flashed a flicker of shame that he was going to erase now and forever. Rising, he got rid of his boots, then slipped the button free on his jeans and eased down the zipper. Her gaze traveled down his stomach, the color rising in her face. "Are you watching?"

She licked her lips. "Yes."

He shoved his pants down. His cock sprang out, fully erect. Kicking his pants away, he braced his legs apart. He really had her attention now. Right on his cock, making his dick twitch and jerk. Logan laid his hand on her cheek. With his other hand, his guided her fingers to his throbbing shaft. "See that? Feel it? That's what you do to me." He couldn't stop from thrusting into her soft, warm hand. Shivers raced down his back. But he kept his eyes opened, letting her see how much he wanted her. Tilting her face up, he leaned close and kissed her. "There's no shame between us, sweetheart. If you want this, then don't be afraid to let me see, feel, and taste how much you want me. Just like I'm showing you."

She stroked the sensitive underside, nearly driving him to his toes, but he stayed flat footed, letting her explore. "Two things."

"Yeah?" He hoped he could hear her over the blood roaring in his ears. The way she was touching him was erotic torture.

"You're huge."

Okay, that slapped a smug smile on his face and unleashed pride in his chest.

She released his dick, pressed back into the couch and hooked her fingers in the top of her panties. "And I want you." Once she dragged that scrap of material off she leaned back.

"Show me."

Becky spread her thighs open. His blood was pounding and need hammered down his spine. He dropped to his knees. "That…Christ. You could kill a man with a mouth-watering surprise like that." His sweet girl was completely bare, her folds swollen and wet for him.

"Birthday present."

"What?" The words didn't make sense. Nothing did, except the driving need to taste her, then bury himself into her until they were both exhausted and satisfied.

"On my birthday, Ava took me for a wax job. Hurt like a bitch. I almost killed her."

"Becky?" Logan grabbed a condom from his pocket and rolled it on.

"Mmm?"

Her legs trembled as he spread her thighs wider with his shoulders. The scent of her arousal saturated his lungs. He flicked his gaze up. "I'll make it better, baby. I'll make it so good, you'll scream when you come."

. . .

Logan's heated gaze between her legs made her feel cherished and sexy in a way nothing else ever had. His warm breath heated her flesh. Shivers danced through her, and her nipples tingled.

Then he leaned in and licked her, igniting her body on fire. She couldn't stay still. Every lick inflamed her more.

Logan clamped a hand on her hip, holding her in place. He rolled his eyes up to watch her as he closed his mouth around her clit.

Shuddering, she couldn't look away from the intensity of his gaze. He traced her opening with his finger tip then eased it in. The slide of his knuckles tore a moan from her.

He flicked the flat of his tongue against her bundle of nerves. Worked in a second finger, finding that spot again. "Oh…" Only his hand on her hips and his eyes on her kept her in place.

Tension built higher and tighter. She writhed and panted, undulating in helpless need. Riding his fingers and mouth, losing all sense of time and place. Desperate, she latched onto his hair trying to get relief. The intensity seared her, should have embarrassed her except for the way he looked at her.

As if she were the center of his universe.

He twisted his fingers, flinging her into an explosion.

Hot, fierce waves of pleasure ripped through her. Becky couldn't hold his gaze and dropped her head back. She crested, shuddering beneath the waves.

"I've got you." Warm arms picked her up and cradled her. With her face pressed against his chest, skin to skin, his hand stroked her back. "Do you know how gorgeous you are? How good you taste?" He kept talking to her, praising her until she settled. She'd never experienced anything like it.

"That was intense."

He lifted her chin, his smile tight. "I almost lost control and came like a teenager before I even got inside you."

His cock pulsed against her hip. "Yeah, we should do something about that."

He sucked in a breath. "Oh we're going to."

His voice rasped with bare restraint, yet he just held her. His generosity touched her, and she rose up on her knees, straddling him. The condom didn't disguise the length and girth of his erection. Becky traced her finger over his plum-colored head, and skated down.

Tendons popped out on his neck and jaw. Getting a hold on her hips, he feathered a finger over her sensitive clit.

A tiny spasm rippled. Becky sucked in a breath as a yawning ache opened between her thighs. Hissing, she grabbed onto his shoulder.

"Need more?" His light eyes stayed on her face as he teased her with soft touches.

It wasn't enough. Her stomach muscles clenched. "Yes. Want it."

"Hold on to me." He grabbed his cock and pressed the head against her. "Take me, sugar."

She eased down, her body stretching as she bore onto him. The most delicious burn tunneled in.

Logan's hands bracketed her hips, stopping her descent. He held her immobilized. "Slow. It's been awhile for you."

He believed her. The last of her fear that he'd think she was a woman who jumped into bed with anyone vanished. Her belly flooded with the sensation of being safe and sexy. Cared for. Her muscles softened, taking more of him.

He pushed up, then pulled out in light, shallow strokes, while holding her immobile. Her thighs bunched with the need to slam down. Take all of him.

"More?"

"Please."

Quirking his full mouth, he drew one of her nipples into his mouth. Streaks of heat arrowed through her and he plunged a bit deeper. She widened her thighs, desperate to be completely filled, but he held back.

His focus lasered in on her as he licked her nipples, driving her higher. The muscles in his shoulders quivered, Becky could feel him resisting the urge to let himself go and take her hard. Instead, he concentrated on building her pleasure back up. As hot as that was, she wanted Logan to lose himself like she had.

Gripping his hair, she tugged him from her breast. "Stop holding back. I can take it." She wanted him to let go like she had.

His muscles froze as he went utterly still. They stared at each other for one beat. In the next second, he flipped her to her back. His face went stark, jaw clamped, muscles corded, and raw need sparked in his eyes. Logan uncensored loomed over her—and he meant to take her.

"Yes." She clutched at him. "Like this."

Hooking an arm beneath her leg, he lifted her and surged in deep. Hitting nerves she didn't know she had. Before she could get her breath, he pulled out and drove back in. Possessive and demanding. His eyes blazed as he powered into her.

She'd done this to him, shattered his control. Adrenaline and wild wanting exploded in her. Becky responded instinctively, shoving her hips up to meet his thrusts, taking everything he gave her. Sweat coated their bodies. The tension expanded within her until she couldn't breathe. She dug her fingers into his skin.

Logan pulled her leg higher, changed the angle and slammed into her, triggering her orgasm. Lights flashed as hot spasms gripped her. He buried his face into her neck, coming hard, his body jerking deep inside her while panting against her skin. She lost track of everything except the waves of pleasure and the scent and feel of Logan. Finally, he slid from her body, flipped them again so she was laying on him.

She forced one hand up to push off.

"Stay." He wrapped her in his arms. "Let me hold you."

His heart thumped against her cheek. "It's okay if you want me to move. You don't have to do this."

He stroked her hair, down her back, over the curve of her ass. Then he slapped her butt.

"Hey." It barely stung.

"Don't use me. A man has his pride. You have to lay here in my arms and act like you want me for more than my amazing cock."

Oh God. When their marriage was over, she was sure to be left with a broken heart.

Chapter Ten

Well hell, this was going to be awkward. Shooting a death glare at the car sitting next to Pam's in his driveway, Logan wondered if some kind of invitation had gone out for everyone in the state to drop by his house.

Becky headed up the porch steps. "That car wasn't here when we left."

Taking in the sight of her butt in those jeans, he tried to focus. "No."

She glanced back at him, her eyes curious. "Do you recognize it?"

"Yep." He took her hand. "Kendra Edwards. She's a friend of the family and runs the *Heart of Texas* e-zine. She often does features on the ranch."

"Friend of the family, or a personal friend?"

He rubbed the back of his neck. "Both." She didn't need to know the details.

"Ah, that kind of friend. Okay." She reached for the

door.

Logan tugged her back. "Our fathers are long-time friends. Kendra's always been around. We just fell into bed a couple times. Now it's over, it was nothing." Right there in front of his eyes, the light in her gaze died and the bounce in her step deflated.

"Nothing. Got it." She slipped through the door before he could stop her.

He was an ass. Telling her it was nothing made her think what they'd had today was nothing. Wrong—it'd been something so special, he didn't have a name for it. Becky wasn't a woman he could have sex with and forget about.

Frustrated, he went in.

"Logan, there you are." Kendra sashayed up to him in skin-tight white pants. "So nice to see you again."

"Hello, Kendra." Going to Becky, he settled his arm around her shoulders, trying to ease her discomfort. "This is my wife, Becky."

"Becky, lovely to meet you." Kendra turned her gaze on Logan. "Your father wants a spread in the e-zine of you all with the horses to showcase both the ranch and the Knights. And I'll be covering the barbeque celebrating your marriage." She strolled up and smiled at Becky. "It's my job to introduce you to Texas society and help you make a good impression."

"Why?"

Kendra arched an eyebrow. "The Knight Ranch is the premier horse ranch in all of Texas."

Becky glanced up at him. "You have cattle, too."

Pleased the she remembered what he'd told her, Logan answered, "Yep, but our reputation is centered around our

Quarter horses. We breed the best and we have a superior training program for the animals. Rodeo competitors come from all over to buy our stock."

"Exactly, and the Knights need to stay in the public eye," Kendra added. "It's part of the business to keep visible in society. As a Knight now, you need to represent the family and ranch."

Logan tugged Becky closer to his side. "You're laying it on a little thick. It's not like we're royalty."

Kendra smiled. "Almost, but we'll bring Becky in as a Cinderella story. The poor girl meets her Knight."

"Oh barf," Pam said.

"No. We're not going to make Becky look like a charity case. Let's go with the truth. Becky and I met through Lucinda. We became friends then married."

"Why so fast at a courthouse with no one there?"

Logan honed in on the kid lying on Becky's shoulder. The baby lifted her head and stared at him. Her eyes dominated her round little face, shimmering with lively curiosity. She reached out her fist, smacking him in the chest. "For Sophie. We wanted to create a stable home for her."

Becky smiled at him, and for a few seconds, he felt like a prince.

"Okay, that could work. I have an idea. Becky, can you ride?"

"A little bit, but not like I imagine Logan and his family does."

She could? He whipped his head around. Hell, he'd never asked her if she could ride. Did she want to? Come to think of it, she'd been excited to see his horses, which he still hadn't shown her since he'd been too busy getting her naked.

She went on as if he wasn't staring at her. "I won some lessons. Enough to stay in a saddle for a little bit."

Kendra beamed. "We'll do a spread of you guys riding, with Logan holding Sophie. It'll be perfect. Readers will see Logan showing his stepdaughter her world now that her mother married a Knight."

Hold the baby? White noise filled his head, memories pushed and shoved. Logan stilled, concentrating on breathing, forcing air in and out of his tight lungs.

I'm in my house, on my land. Not in Afghanistan racing against time to find the underground girl's school before the faction of the Taliban did.

The pressure in his skull ratcheted up and up. A hand slipped beneath his shirt and curved around his side.

Becky pressed into his ribs. "Can you do it?"

Her touch and voice shoved back the flashback. He honed in on her like an anchor. Her soft eyes shimmered with concern for him. He needed to do this. "We'll try it."

Sophie began to fuss and squirm in her arms. "She's hungry. I have to feed her."

He latched onto that as an excuse. "We'll firm up the details later." He showed Kendra and Pam out, then dropped into the chair. Becky fed the baby on the couch, the contented sounds of the baby eating filling the room. Sophie got a fist full of Becky's hair and studied her mom's face. Becky angled her head down, her brown eyes glowing with love as she wrapped her hand around her child's.

Earlier today, she'd been his lover, so fiercely hot he'd lost himself in her. And now she was a mom, so tender with her love for Sophie, she made him ache. The sight of them chased out ugliness and horror in his brain.

Becky met his gaze. "Are you going to be able to do this?"

"Hold Sophie?" He couldn't fail them. "I have to." It'd look strange if he constantly avoided the baby. Another thought occurred to him: this was Becky's child they were talking about, the baby she loved more than anything in the world. "I won't drop her or let her get hurt."

She shook her head. "I'm not worried about that. Pam assured me Sophie is safe with you on a horse. I'll be there too, and believe me, I'll stop something if I think it's unsafe for Sophie. But I'm talking about you. If you can't do it, just let me know. I'll make a scene, do the mom freak out, claiming it scares me too much to have her on a horse. That way you're not put on the spot."

"You'd do that?" Didn't she consider him weak to be afraid of a baby?

Once she shifted Sophie to her shoulder, she patted her back. "I don't want you to do this then end up spending the night on the front porch unable to come in the house."

Was she protecting him? That was insane. He was supposed to protect her and her child. "I'll handle it." He stood up. "I'll start some dinner then I have work to do."

"Okay, but Logan?"

He paused, once more captivated as she settled Sophie to her other breast. "Yeah?"

She tilted her head back to fix her gaze on him. "While I'm here, you don't have to handle it alone."

• • •

Becky was nearly as nervous as when she used to go onstage

in pageants. It was just a photo shoot. She'd done a ton of them. But the truth was she didn't want to look bad for Logan. She might be his temporary wife, but she wanted him to be proud of her.

Oh girl, you're in so much trouble!

Okay, not love…but she liked him, as well as his stepmom and Pam. Glancing at Kendra with her sassy dark red hair falling to her chin, waist-length fitted jacket paired with jeans and boots Becky would have to win the lottery to own, she wished she had on something a little nicer.

Oh enough. Her scalloped ivory top, jeans, and scuffed cowboy boots would have to do. At least she'd spent quality time with her curling iron and makeup. Besides, Sophie looked adorable in her pink hair ribbon, matching shirt, and little jeans. She focused on that as they crossed the grass of the pasture.

When they got closer to the two saddled horses waiting for them, Sophie let out a squeal. Becky had her facing out on her hip, and the baby shrieked in excitement, her arms and legs bouncing.

"Someone's eager." Logan settled his heavy arm across Becky's shoulder.

"I wondered if she'd be afraid."

"Sugar, she's not scared. She's trying to get to the horses." He waved to Kendra and headed to where Pam held the big animals. "This gray is Gemma, she's a gentle girl."

Becky had to hold Sophie's arms to keep her from batting the horse.

"Here." Pam took the baby's hand and helped her pet the horse's head.

Gemma blew a little air out her nostrils, and looked at

Sophie.

Her baby giggled and squirmed, her whole body radiating joy as she tried to pet her again. For a second, Becky was thrust back in time, watching her older brother so excited at the rodeo. "Tyler loved horses. Didn't have an ounce of fear, while I was scared."

Warm arms came around her. "Looks like Sophie's got some of her uncle in her."

That made her smile. To have a little piece of her brother in her baby was like a precious gift. "Good. Tyler was braver than me." She didn't want her daughter to be afraid; she wanted her safe and loved.

Logan tightened his arms. "You're braver than you think. You had a baby on your own."

She looked up into his eyes. "That wasn't bravery, that was love. As soon as I realized I was pregnant, she was mine."

His gaze darkened, while his hand spread on her belly. Everything around them blurred, and all she saw was this man consuming her with his gaze. Then his sister's voice broke the odd spell.

"I can't wait until she's old enough to learn to ride." Pam grinned at them. "I'll teach her to barrel race. She can be a star like her Aunt Pam."

For a few blissful seconds, it was like she and Sophie had a family, surrounded by people who cared.

"We need to get started." Kendra moved up next to them. The lighting is perfect."

Logan tensed behind her.

"I'll hold Sophie, while you get settled." Pam took the baby.

Becky's palms grew damp. Both horses were saddled

and ready. "Am I riding Gemma?" She stroked the horse's nose, then rubbed her neck.

Logan put his hand on her lower back. "Yep. I'll be on Remy." He checked the saddle, the pad, the straps, everything from what Becky could tell. "All set, come here Bec." He held out his hand.

She took it and before she knew it, he had her in the saddle. "Keep your line straight along shoulders, hips, and heels." Quickly Logan corrected her position and gave her the reigns. "Okay?"

"It's coming back to me." All two months' worth of lessons from four or five years ago, and then a couple times at riding stables.

He rested his hand on her calf. "You're doing fine. Your seat and legs give her the most directions. Stay calm and she'll be calm. It usually takes a lot to spook Gemma."

"Got it." She wasn't going to screw this up.

"Pam, can you hang onto Sophie for a few minutes?" He moved to his horse, a tall black animal that he greeted before doing the same saddle check routine he'd done with Gemma. Once finished, he swung up with such fluid grace it took her breath away. How could a tall, muscled man move like that?

Logan titled his chin toward Pam. "I'm going to have Becky walk a bit and get used to her mount."

"Watch your mama, Sophie." Pam turned the baby, and Becky waved at her daughter.

"Bec, relax and focus on riding. Don't look at Sophie. I want you to watch where you're going." He clicked his tongue and his horse flowed into a walk. She followed, using her legs to get the horse to walk, and guiding her with the reins.

"Turn your body the way you want her to go," Pam called out. "Keep it natural, she'll understand."

After a few turns, with both Pam and Logan giving her corrections, she enjoyed the challenge of asking this powerful creature to follow her directions. It was exhilarating. And when Logan praised her for doing something right? Freaking awesome.

Logan brought his horse around to stand by Pam and Kendra. "One more time, Bec. I want to see your control."

Okay, she could do this. Becky concentrated on keeping her body in the straight line, guiding with her legs, seat, and reins. Bringing Gemma to a stop, she let out her breath. "I want to learn more."

"Not today. I got some great shots of the two of you." Kendra nodded at Pam holding Sophie. "Now let's get Logan with the baby. That will be the money shot. The cowboy and former Marine hero holding a baby? Everyone will fall in love."

"Don't call me a hero."

Becky froze in the saddle at Logan's harsh tone.

"Okay, I…" Kendra looked away, a flush crawling up her neck. "I'm sorry."

Logan creaked as he adjusted in his saddle. "Let me have the baby."

Becky sucked in a breath, ready to put a stop to this if either her daughter or Logan wasn't up to doing a stepdad-and-daughter moment on the horse. So far, Sophie hadn't shown an ounce of fear, but Logan hadn't held her yet.

Pam crossed to her brother and lifted the baby. Sophie held her arms up, reaching for Logan. Her face glowed with excitement. She began babbling her joy.

Becky's heart skipped a beat. Her sweet girl wanted Logan.

As Logan closed his hands around her baby, a lingering gentleness chased out the last traces of anger on his face, and erased all worry from Becky's mind.

Her daughter was safe in her stepfather's arms.

It was Becky's heart that was in danger.

· · ·

Logan met those incredible, trusting eyes in her baby face. Then Sophie smiled, revealing her gums. And just like that he was lost. He tried to fight it, tried to resist. If he took her, this little girl was going to rip all the carefully constructed Band-Aids off his wounds, leaving him exposed and vulnerable. If he made the wrong choice and Sophie got hurt, it'd shred him into a living mass of bloody pain and endless nightmares. He closed his hands around Sophie and lifted her. She was so light and tiny. His hands circled all the way around her, his fingers touching.

Don't squeeze too tight.

Logan sat frozen, holding the baby out like a squirming puppy. She kicked her little legs, a huge smile carving her face. Her hazel eyes stared at him with complete trust. Remembering to breathe, he inhaled her powdery baby scent.

A memory washed across his mind—Pammy when she was about four or five, pretending to run from him as he pounded across the pasture atop his horse. Logan would lean over and easily sweep her up. She'd throw her arms around his neck, laughing with the wild abandonment of a child.

Okay, if he could do that when he'd been a teenager, he could hold a baby on his horse. "Let's do this."

The kid babbled something, as if agreeing. She held her pudgy arms out to him. Her fingers were so tiny, maybe half the length of his little finger. It'd be so easy to break her. He carefully tucked her into his the crook of his arm.

Don't hold her too tight, but tight enough to not drop her.

The constant directions from his brain were making him clench his jaw hard enough to hear a popping sound in his ear. He glanced down. Sophie gave him another gummy grin and bounced.

Damned if he didn't smile back. How could he help it, this kid had no fear. None. She wanted to ride. He urged Remy into a walk.

Sophie giggled, craning her head back and forth to see everything. Her small body wiggled in unrestrained happiness. Logan could imagine her in a few years—a girl with Becky's blond hair on her own horse tearing across the pastures.

He grinned…until the picture in his head changed, and all he saw was that baby in the mud house….

Focus. He wasn't in Afghanistan. He was in the saddle on his ranch where he had control.

Turning, he headed toward Becky. She'd dismounted and leaned a shoulder against the tree. Her beaming smile hit him square in the chest, like an anchor, that grin held him right here in the present.

"Hold up," Kendra said. "Act like you're showing your stepdaughter the land and her heritage now that she's a

Knight."

He'd practically forgotten Kendra. She was running around, snapping pictures. Okay, he could do a few more minutes. Logan stopped Remy, then carefully shifted Sophie, and leaned his head close, pointing off into the distance as if he were showing the kid something.

"What's wrong?"

Pammy's sharp voice jerked his attention to his sister and wife by the tree. What the hell?

Becky was dancing frantically and waving her arms around her body. "Bees! There's bees."

"Crap, a hive." Pam got the horse's reins and led her away.

Logan went on alert. A ticked off hive was dangerous. He opened his mouth to tell his wife to calm down and move away when Becky whirled around and ran. What the hell was she over-reacting for? That wasn't like her.

"Logan!" Pam screamed. "Becky says she's allergic to bee stings!"

Allergic. He hadn't known. "Shit."

Becky's long legs ate up ground as she fled. He couldn't see if any bees followed her. Then he heard her yelp. Stung or hurt in another way? Thrusting Sophie into Kendra's arms, he said, "Get the first aid kit in my truck." He urged Remy into a run. The horse responded, easily covering the ground. As he closed in on Becky, he heard her panting over the pounding hooves. "Becky, stop!"

She kept running in a full-blown panic. Fear that she'd trip and break her leg spurred him into action. Once he caught up to her, he leaned low, hooked his arm around her waist, and hoisted her up. "Swing your leg over."

Becky latched onto him, wheezing. She was straddling him, her arms around his neck, face buried against his shoulder. "It's okay, baby. Hang on." He slowed and turned the horse, heading straight for the truck. Hot fear burned his veins. What did he do? Call the paramedics? Take her to the hospital? He threw Pam the reins.

"Look at me." He eased Becky's head back.

Her face was beet red, eyes swollen and wet from crying. Jesus, she was terrified. Then her eyes widened. "Sophie! She could be allergic, too!"

Pam put her hand on Becky's leg. "She's safe in the truck with Kendra."

Becky relaxed a little bit, but she was definitely struggling to get air.

"Did you get stung, or just scared?"

She held up her arm. "Stung. Purse in truck. Throat's swelling. Injection."

Jesus Christ. Logan saw at least four or five welts on her arm. Alarm fired in his guts and chest. Dismounting with her in his arms was tricky, but he got them on the ground and to the truck. Yanking open the passenger door, he set Becky down. He grabbed her purse off the floorboard and fished out the injection pen. Snapping off the cap, he caught her face. Her eyes were dialed with raw panic. "Thigh?"

She barely nodded.

No time to think, he plunged the needle into her leg, then picked her up, and cradled her on her lap. "Breathe, Becky. Nice and easy."

"Paramedics are on their way." Pam's blue eyes were worried as hell. She had a pair of tweezers from the first aid kit. "Hold her arm."

While his sister worked to get the stingers out, he pitched his voice low and soothing. "You're okay. Just breathe." Her body was rigid, but he could hear air moving.

Thank God the paramedics arrived fast. They slapped oxygen on her and Logan gently settled her on the gurney, all the while his thoughts raced. Had he been fast enough with the shot? An anaphylactic reaction could be fatal. "You're okay, sugar. Just relax."

Becky fought, yanking the oxygen off. "Sophie."

A second wave of alarm spread through him. He'd be alone with the kid. He could hear the baby crying in his truck. What the hell would he do?

One look at Becky's frantic eyes told him what a selfish bastard he was. He pressed the oxygen back on her face and held her hands in his. Her painful wheezing tore at him, and he firmed his voice. "We'll take care of her, I swear it. I'll meet you at the hospital. Just do what they tell you."

"We need to go. Now."

He saw the young paramedic's concern. They had the equipment in the vehicle to help her. Logan would only be in the way. It took everything he had, but he let her go.

Once the ambulance left, he spun and headed toward his truck. Kendra had climbed out of the vehicle, and both she and Pam were desperately trying to calm Sophie. The sirens had terrorized her.

Pam looked up at him. "She wants her mom. Maybe you can try holding her?"

He stared at the kid's red face, her huge eyes flooded in heartbreaking tears. That baby loved her mama more than anything in the world. He should have known his wife was severely allergic. Should have moved quicker, gotten to

Becky faster.

Sophie arched back from Pam and reached her arms out to Logan. For a second, time stopped. All he saw in that desperate baby was longing for him to make it all better. Fix it. His pulse hammered, his heart stuttered. He couldn't breathe as the familiar panic banded around his chest, squeezing tighter and tighter.

Escape. He had to escape.

Forcing his lungs to work, he croaked out, "I have to get to the hospital. Take Sophie to my house. Jiggy's there, maybe seeing the dog will calm her." He raced off. In his rearview mirror, he saw the baby bury her face in Pam's neck, her entire body shuddering with sobs.

His wife was in an ambulance fighting a severe allergic reaction and he'd just bailed on his inconsolable stepdaughter. Did he need any more proof as to why he couldn't have a real marriage and family?

Right now, what mattered the most was getting to Becky.

Chapter Eleven

Grateful to be out of the hospital, Becky ignored her fatigue and achiness. The epinephrine shot had kicked in when she'd been in the ambulance, along with the IV they gave her, so she had stabilized quickly. Once home, she managed to get her exhausted and cranky daughter asleep. The shower had made Becky feel much better. With her hair wet, and wearing a tank and sweat pants, she padded barefoot to the kitchen.

Logan's green eyes hit hers and she stopped, slapping her hand down on the table. Her stomach flipped, and heat warmed her chest. The memory of her wild panic as she'd run from the bees, then Logan's arm coming around her and yanking her off her feet tripped her replay button. It had been his eyes, his voice, his touch that had eased her terror and soothed her frantic worry. He'd stayed by her side at the hospital. Held her hand.

And Becky had fallen in love. Wholly and completely.

With a man who only wanted her temporarily to get his land. Smart, Becky, real smart. But what did she do now? How did she figure out a way to protect her heart?

"Feeling better?"

Crap, she stared at him like a moron. "Yes." Except for her tight skin, tingling breasts, and the throbbing between her legs that was creating an edgy need to strip off her clothes and beg him to take her, possess her, drive them both to wild heights so she could feel safe and alive, not so damned scared and struggling to breathe.

"Come sit down and have dinner. Just soup and sandwiches. Eating at the island okay with you?"

Right, dinner. Not wild, hot sex to ease that frantic ache building in her. Nodding, she forced her feet to take her to a barstool. Logan slid a bowl of steaming soup in front of her, then added a thick grilled cheese sandwich. The scent of toasted bread and oozing cheese woke her stomach up. Better. Craving food helped take her mind off her supersized sex drive.

"Is your arm sore?"

He missed nothing, like the fact she was eating with her left hand. "A little bit. Most of the swelling is down though."

He could love you. Maybe if you figure out what he wants...

No, that was the old Becky who had found herself pregnant, involved in a hit-and-run, and now fighting to keep her child. Besides, Logan had been clear what he wanted—

No children.

No matter how it had looked today when he'd held Sophie on that horse. That moment when his eyes met hers...Logan didn't want children or a wife. He wanted his land, and to start and be a part of Camp Warrior Recovery. He was going to help a lot of men and women who deserved his passion and caring.

And she was going to let him go.

But for right now, tonight? She wanted him, no she *needed* him. Needed his arms around her, his body filling hers and pushing out the lingering terror. But she was going to keep her lines clear—it was sex, not love. The old Becky would cling after sex, struggling to form that bond she craved. This Becky wasn't going to do that. They'd have sex and she'd go back to her room. Keep the lines clear. No emotional entanglements.

"You should have told me you were allergic."

That jerked her from her thoughts. "It never came up."

Logan swiveled on the stool until he faced her. "You could have died. Why the hell haven't you seen an allergist like the doctors told you to today?" Fury throbbed in the vein in his temple.

"We didn't have health insurance. In college my mom nagged me to do it, and I was just going to start them when I got pregnant, then mom got sick…" She shrugged. "Something else always took priority."

"Bullshit. Nothing takes priority over your health. You're going this week."

She narrowed her eyes, ready for a fight. Anything to stop feeling this driving need. "Don't start ordering me around."

"Do you want Sophie to grow up without her mother?"

"No."

"Then don't argue. This isn't about money, your life could be at stake."

"Fine." She slid off the stool, gathered up her dishes, and went to the sink. "Thank you." It was time to get some distance.

Logan's image appeared in the window over the sink as he came up behind her. His gaze captured hers in the darkened glass. "You're tired and a bit edgy."

She gripped the edge of the counter. "You're right. I'm sorry I didn't tell you about my allergy and for flipping out today." It took all her will to not look down. "I ran like a lunatic."

"You're allergic. No one could blame you for panicking."

"I'll clean up. You've done enough today and there's no one here now. We don't need to pretend."

Logan slapped his hands down on the counter, caging her. His front pressed against her back. "What does that mean?"

"We have a deal. Nothing but a deal."

"Keep going."

"I need lines."

"Lines." He said the word like it was a new concept.

"We have to live together. In front of people you have to act like you care. I get that. You saved my life today and arranged for Sophie's care. I'm grateful." Her throat thickened. Becky dug her hand into the counter.

"Are you saying that I would have left you to die if we'd been alone?"

"Of course not. Don't be ridiculous." This wasn't his fault and she needed to be straight with him. "Look, it's me, okay? I'm not going to be able to resist you." His eyes reflected in the window were a magnetic force that compelled her attention. "Even now, I want you. God, I want you." She needed his arms around her, but she needed to protect herself at the same time.

He covered her hands with his. "Baby, if you want me, I'm right here." He brushed her damp hair aside, and kissed her neck.

Shivers fanned out from every spot his warm mouth touched. Her nipples peaked and pleasure traveled lower. He spread his hand out on her belly, fanning her desperation to sink into him, to feel alive and not alone. But she would be alone again. Her stomach tightened. "No, wait." She had to have some controls in place or she'd end up begging him to love her at the end of this deal, instead of gracefully letting him go.

He lifted his head, meeting her eyes in the window.

"I need to keep this separate. Sex is just sex. When we want it, we do it."

"With you so far."

"But I'm not sleeping with you. I'm not staying all night in your bed and confusing things. It's just sex. Nothing more."

His eyes hardened. "It's more."

Wanting to belong to someone, to have a safe place in a scary world ballooned in her until she could barely breathe. "The forever kind of more?"

Logan sucked in a breath. "No."

The longing shriveled in shame. Why had she done that? Asked such a pathetic needy question when she knew the answer? Struggling to be strong, she said, "Then it's just sex. For once in my life, I'm going to be smart and learn the difference."

His body went rigid. Ice coated his gaze.

"When we're around others, we'll pretend. Alone we'll

concentrate on our goals. You developing Camp Warrior Recovery, and me on Sophie and getting my degree."

"And having sex." He snapped each word.

"Meaningless sex." Her brain rebelled, tapping out warnings. This wasn't like her, not even close, but she refused to listen. It was time for her to grow up and accept that happily-ever-after was a fairy tale.

"That's what you want?"

No. She wanted it all—a real marriage, a life partner who had her back. But that wasn't going to happen between them. "Yes."

Logan kept stroking her arm, sending tingles up and down with each pass.

"But you won't sleep in my bed, won't let me hold you, give you the tenderness you deserve?"

She was too weak. Just like she'd done a second ago—wanting to believe he'd love her, really love her. The terror of today had been too much and she wanted to cling to Logan, but she couldn't. "No."

"All right." His hands went to her waist. He caught hold of her sweatpants and panties. While watching her with anger sharpening his eyes, he tugged them down to her knees.

"What are you doing?" She was exposed from her belly to her knees.

"We don't need a bed for this. No one is here. No one can see us. If you want meaningless sex, I'll give it to you." He pulled her back against his chest and brushed her skin from one hip bone to the other. Turning her chin, he asked, "Is kissing allowed?"

Confusion overwhelmed her. He was cold and mad, yet she could feel his erection pressing against her back. She longed for his hands on her, hated the distance between them. "Yes but—"

His mouth crashed over hers and she could taste his anger. His hand slipped beneath her shirt, tweaking her nipple creating more paths of fire. Then his hand dipped between her thighs.

Logan used his foot to push her feet apart. The sweatpants around her knees kept her pinned. She was being taken. Possessed. But not loved or cared for. Not even tenderness.

Methodically, he parted her damp folds and teased, sliding back and forth over her clit until she ached and moaned into his mouth. He pulled back, his face a mask. "Good enough. I'll get a condom and be right back." He walked away.

Leaving her cold. Humiliated. Hot tears burned. Becky stood in his kitchen with her pants shoved to her knees. She yanked them up and ran to her room. Shutting the door, her heart pounded. He'd been willing to give it to her exactly as she'd demanded. Crawling onto the bed, she yanked the pillow to her chest and buried her face in it as her tears poured out. She didn't want to wake her baby with her sobbing.

Or worse, let Logan hear her.

• • •

Logan slapped his hands on his low dresser and stared at himself in the mirror.

There was no excuse for what he'd just done out there. Becky had been through hell today. She was having a reaction to nearly dying. He'd seen her eyes when she'd struggled to breathe—she'd been fucking terrified. And he decided now was the time to teach her a lesson about what meaningless sex really was. Never in his life had he treated a woman like that. Ever.

He heard her run into her room and shut the door. Not slam it, but ease it closed. Logan hung his head. She wasn't the only one having a reaction. She'd scared the hell out of him today, and he'd taken it out on her, because he wanted her in his bed, needed to feel her alive, to know he hadn't screwed up and let her die. And yeah, he'd wanted sex, but not like that.

He faced his reflection. Part of him wanted to get out of the house and take off. Just get some space. Go sleep in the trailer. But he couldn't leave her like that. He'd humiliated her, hurt her when she'd already been hurting.

Logan pushed off the dresser. He walked to her room and opened the door.

"Go away. Please."

Her voice crackled with tears. The light spilling in from the door showed him Becky on her side with her knees drawn up, hugging her pillow. He went in, glanced in the crib. The baby slept on her back, her face sweet and peaceful. She was fine, but her mother needed care and he couldn't do it in here. Logan went to the bed, leaned down and lifted Becky.

"No." It came out a sob.

"I'm not leaving you alone." He carried her to his room, killed the lights, and put her in his bed. Stripping to his boxers, he slid in and tucked her into his arms.

She burrowed into him, her body shaking.

"Go ahead, baby. Let it out." He rubbed her back as she

cried. "You didn't deserve to be treated like that." All he'd had to do was pick her up, take her to his bed, and make love to her as many times as they'd both needed to know that she was alive and safe. Then let her go sleep in the room with her child. Hell it even made sense.

It just felt wrong.

Becky was not the kind of woman a man kicked out of his bed. She was a woman a man did everything in his power to keep there.

She quieted, and he thought maybe she'd settle in and fall asleep.

"I'm afraid."

He tilted her head to see her face in the thin moonlight. Her tears had stopped, but her face was swollen. Using the edge of the sheet, he wiped away the remnants of her tears. "Why?" He hoped to God she could still trust him. Okay, probably not to have sex with him, what he'd done was unforgiveable, but she could talk to him.

"I was so scared today, then you held me and calmed me down. I'm afraid I'm going to need you too much. Then you'll be gone."

He sucked in a breath. "Like your father and brother?"

It took her a moment to answer. "I was supposed to put my shoes on before I went outside, but I didn't, and went out to play in the yard. I stepped on a bee. My mom had to take me to the hospital. When we got back, the house was on fire."

His chest burned like he'd been branded.

"Bees freak me out now. My mom never blamed me. My dad and Tyler were welding something in the garage, and somehow the fire started. I know that now, I get it. If my mom and I had been there, I don't know that anything would have been different. I understand that."

"But you don't always believe it." Just like he knew he wasn't back in Afghanistan standing inside that house that doubled as a school for girls, but sometimes…he believed he was. Not as much these days, but yeah, he got it.

"Not always. I couldn't control my fear today when the bees came out of their hive. I'm sorry." She pushed her face into his chest.

Logan stroked her hair. "Nothing to be sorry for, baby. Not a thing." He kept proving over and over why he wasn't cut out for marriage or having a family of his own. Becky had needed him to make love to her, give her that connection that made them feel alive and valued.

And he'd decided he'd humiliate her and teach her a lesson.

"Listen to me, sweetheart. I'm here. I can't be the husband you deserve, but I'll be your friend even when this is over. You need a man's arms around you, you come to me. I'll hold you as long as you need me too." Logan was never going to have a woman and family of his own, so he could give Becky this. In time, she wouldn't need him anymore. She'd find a man worthy of her.

"You'd do that?"

Her breath whispered across his chest like a caress. He held her tighter, trying to give her comfort. "Yes." He tucked his hand beneath her shirt, spreading his fingers behind her lungs. He needed to feel her breathing. "You're safe. I swear it. Go to sleep and I'll put you back in your bed." Just as soon as he could let go of her.

It was after midnight before he could make himself do

it. When he settled her in her bed, and walked out, loneliness closed around him like a fist, stealing his breath.

When this was over, he'd have his land…but would that be an empty victory without Becky in his life?

. . .

"The good news is the judge has denied Dylan access to Sophie until the trial to determine who gets possession and visitation." Felicia Redding folded her hands on her desk.

Relieved, Becky glanced at Logan. Her lawyer had requested that he be here today.

He met her gaze. "See, sweetheart? I told you. Nothing to worry about."

"There's more news."

Becky turned back. "Good, bad?"

Felicia's eyes appeared to be measuring them. "The judge has ordered home study."

"What does that mean?" And why did the lawyer keep examining them like they were on trial?

"A social worker will be assigned to the case, and will evaluate Sophie's home life by conducting a series of interviews with both sides. That will mean you, your husband…" She paused, her eyes hard on Logan. "Both your families, references, and some third parties. Everything will be looked at."

Becky gripped the wooden arms of the chair. "Uh, Logan's family is just getting to know us. Right now his sister, Pam, is babysitting Sophie."

Felicia tapped a pen on her desk. "This marriage is rather sudden. When you were here a few weeks ago, you never mentioned it."

Did she look like a deer in headlights?

"I hadn't asked her to marry me then." Logan reached over and took her hand. "I was waiting because Becky's mom had been sick and just passed. But when I found out that Dylan was harassing Becky, my plans changed immediately."

"If that's the truth, then we don't have a problem. But if you're hiding something and this marriage is exposed as anything else…" She honed in on Becky. "You will lose custody."

Her mouth went absolutely dry. It'd been just over a week since the bee sting. Logan had treated Becky with kindness, but they hadn't so much as kissed. It was just too… awkward she guessed. They'd both focused on their goals, basically seeing each other at dinner, and the couple of times Logan took her riding to improve her skills.

They didn't have a marriage. They had a roommate agreement, which was fine—unless they were discovered and she lost Sophie.

Chapter Twelve

Logan stopped his horse waiting for Becky to catch up to him and Sophie. The baby squirmed, her bottom lip pushing out in a clear statement. Unable to resist, he chuckled. "Hang on there, half pint." He nudged his horse into turning a circle. Sophie bounced and kicked her legs, fully approving.

With the baby quiet for a minute, he watched as Becky guided Gemma up to them. Damn, she looked good on her mount. She still had a ways to go to be able to keep up with him, but her seat was natural and the glow in her face told him she loved it. The thought of riding full out with Becky, tearing across the pastures, laughing... *Don't go there.* They only had a short time together, then he had to let her go. And after he'd hurt her with that stunt he'd pulled a week ago, Logan tried to keep his hands off her. Every day was harder though, he ached to hold her, kiss her. He missed that intimacy he had with Becky.

Stopping Gemma next to him, she smiled at her baby

then lifted her gaze to him. "You doing okay?"

That right there was exactly what he meant. Despite her fear that she'd lose her baby, she was concerned that holding Sophie might trigger his PTSD. "I can control it as long as I'm outside." The low grade anxiety was there, like a fly following him. Right now, focusing on getting his father on their side in the custody battle helped.

Not a chance in hell he'd let his old man see him struggling with flashbacks or anxiety.

Sophie fussed and squirmed, tired of waiting.

Becky's eyes crinkled at the corners, and she leaned over to stroke Sophie's arm. "Hope that impresses your dad."

Those sweet gestures of love between Bec and her baby might look small to someone else, but to him, they were huge. That constant reassurance that Sophie was loved, cherished, and protected. This kid would never wake in the morning to find her mother had vanished.

He shut down that line of thought and answered her question as he nudged Remy into a walk. "Trust me, this will work. When he sees how much she loves horses, he'll support us in the custody battle."

She guided her horse next to him. "That easy?"

His neck tensed. "It's never easy with him. Most kids are a little afraid of a horse the first time they see them."

"What was it like when you first saw a horse?"

"I refused to get anywhere near it." He'd never seen a horse up close before, and it scared the piss out of him.

"Was Brian mad?"

"Disgusted. He refused to have a sniveling coward for a son. He dragged me in the training ring with all the ranch hands watching—" He clamped his jaw closed.

"That was cruel." Outrage cut through her voice.

"Long time ago, Bec. It doesn't matter."

But that fact that she cared...yeah that mattered to him. A lot more than he wanted to admit.

Oh, it mattered, Becky thought as she kept pace next to Logan and Sophie. What had he been, eight? Torn out of his life and thrown into a new one, with no one there he knew? Yet he'd survived, and mastered riding horses. But the biggest kicker? Logan wasn't cruel. His father had been so harsh with him, yet Logan was gentle and patient with her.

Her throat tightened with a wave of thick desire to touch and sooth him, to chase out the lonely certainty that he couldn't love. Or be loved. Logan had erected emotional walls to survive, yet he craved a real connection during sex.

Sex was his way of feeling, and she'd tried to turn it into a meaningless physical encounter to protect her heart. It didn't work. She cared more now than a week ago, so why fight it? Determination seared through her. No more holding back. Instead, she was going to give herself to him completely. And when the time came to split up, she'd let him go and accept the pain.

"That's Abby in the ring on her horse."

Pulling herself out of her thoughts, she concentrated on his sister. Abby's face was shadowed beneath her hat, but her long sinewy body sat perfectly aligned with the saddle while talking to Brian. Logan's father had the same seat on his horse on the side of the ring.

Becky scanned the entire area. "There's a calf in the ring." A little brown guy nosed the fence line.

"Abby's practicing roping. She competes and does demonstrations. She also trains horses for roping and a few other things."

"She's good at roping?"

"Top ranked, but she'd much rather run the ranch."

"Then why does she do it?"

"Abby does everything our father wants in the hopes that one day he'll see her as something more than a showpiece."

Not wanting to be overheard, she let that go. Brian and Abby turned to them as they approached.

Logan stopped his horse close to her. "Becky, this is Abby."

She shifted her gaze to Logan's half sister. Her face was lean, her eyes sharp. "Hi, Abby, nice to meet you."

"You're holding the reins in two hands. Hold them in your left like this." She held up her gloved hand to demonstrate. "Our horses are trained for that."

Becky flushed. "Sorry, I haven't been riding very long. Logan's teaching me."

"Your seat is decent for a beginner. Bring your elbows in slightly, right there. Now position your hand right here in front of the pommel." She demonstrated.

Becky was slightly mesmerized by the woman. Abby's voice wasn't unkind, just factual.

"You're a fast learner. Relax your right arm on your thigh." Once Becky did that, Abby nodded.

"Thanks for the help."

"No problem. The horse will respond better if your seat and handling are familiar to her."

Becky leaned forward and rubbed Gemma's neck. "She's been really patient with me. She doesn't even mind Sophie's excited yells."

Abby's face softened. "She has a forgiving temperament. Logan rescued her, and spent one of his times on leave working with her to gain her trust."

Becky's interest spiked. "Rescue?" She turned to Logan, recalling that he'd told her working with abused or poorly trained horses was his favorite thing.

His jaw clenched. "Bad breaking and training. Those bastards nearly destroyed her spirit. When we got her, her mouth was all torn up. It took a month or two just to get her healthy before I started training her."

Her chest ached for the poor animal. "How can people do that? Look at her. She's so sweet. She even lets Sophie slobber all over her trying to hug her." She had to blink the sick rage from her eyes so she didn't embarrass Logan with her tears in front of his family.

Sophie chose that moment to bounce in Logan's arms and complain.

Becky edged Gemma closer and took her baby's hand. "Brian, this is Sophie. She's my daughter."

"What's she squalling about?"

Logan laughed. "Because we stopped. She wants to ride. Or pet all the horses. Watch." Logan clicked his tongue, and Remy backed up. Within three steps, Sophie quieted. Logan walked the animal, then set him into a jog. In seconds, Sophie laughed and kicked her legs. He brought Remy smoothly back around on Becky's right.

Brian's eyes lit up. "How old is she?"

Pride spread like warm oil through Becky's chest. "Less

than four months. I thought she'd be afraid, but she loves horses. She has Jiggy, our little dog, at home and she adores him, but this surprised me."

Sophie frowned and let out an unhappy sigh.

"Abby," Brian said, "rope the calf. Let's see what the kid does."

Logan's sister lifted the coiled rope off the saddle.

Brian turned to Becky. "Know anything about roping?"

She shook her head while noting her daughter was watching Abby.

"The rope is a lariat. See how she holds the coils with the reins in her left hand? From that she feeds the loop in her right hand to rope the calf." He turned to his daughter. "When you're ready."

Abby and her horse set off. That startled the calf into a run. The horse was incredibly agile, able to follow as the creature darted left and right. While watching the calf and controlling the horse, Abby effortlessly built the loop in her right hand, then twirled it overhead and threw it.

The loop slid around the calf.

Once the calf was in place, Abby got off and freed it while the horse stood still.

"Well, look at that."

Brian's comment tugged Becky's gaze from Abby and she smiled at her daughter. Logan held her high, and Sophie's eyes were glued to the scene in the training ring. Quiet and totally focused.

Brian led his horse out of the ring. "Logan, give the baby to Becky and go rope the calf. See if Sophie watches you."

Becky started to dismount.

"What are you doing?"

Flushing at her father-in-law's sharp question, she grimaced. "I'm not sure I can hold Sophie and keep control of Gemma if something happened."

"She'll see better from the saddle." He turned his gaze. "Sophie, come here darlin'. Let's watch your step-daddy do some real work." He took Sophie from Logan, then eased his horse closer to Becky.

Sophie was more interested in Logan as he got into the ring than who was holding her. Logan took the rope from Abby and showed it to his horse.

"Remy is a good roping horse," Brian said. "Logan is letting him know they'll be working with the lariat. Next he'll warm him up in the ring."

Logan worked that rope like an extension of his hand, while controlling Remy. By the time Logan and Remy chased the calf, they were working as a seamless team while Abby watched.

"Did a little research on your background. Dylan Ridgemont is Sophie's father. You were both involved in a hit-and-run in Austin."

The abrupt comment made her jump. Gemma shifted uneasily, probably trying to figure out what Becky wanted. She calmed the horse, taking a minute to recover. "Yes." Lifting her head, she added, "He didn't want her until he got out of prison."

"Family wants her. If you have her, you can cause them trouble."

"I don't want to cause trouble. I don't want anything from them." She took a breath. Since Brian had asked, it'd be better to tell him all of it now. "We saw our lawyer today, the court is ordering a home study."

His eyebrows shot up. "You're dragging my son into a mess."

The edge in his voice bit deep, but it was also true. "I know. And, by extension, your family. The social worker will want to talk to all of you."

"If you're the real thing, the woman who can keep Logan here where he belongs, taking over the ranch, then I'll support you in the custody battle. But if you're playing on my son's weaknesses, then I'll make sure you lose custody."

Becky sucked in a breath at both the threat and the word "weaknesses." Did Brian know about Logan's PTSD and his struggles? "What weaknesses?"

"He's always been soft, that boy. His mother tried to ruin him." Brian shook his head.

She had the fierce urge to defend her husband. "Logan's strong and knows his own mind."

"Strong is being a man and doing your duty. Not chasing a child's dream and running a camp for men who can't deal with life. He wants to have that as a charity, fine, we can spin it to make it look good. But he needs to take up his birthright of this ranch." He stared hard at Becky. "Your job is to make that happen."

And if she didn't? Fear congealed in her stomach. Sophie looked perfectly safe in his arms atop the horse. Her little girl was so busy watching Logan and Abby team roping the calf, she didn't care who held her. "Are you saying if I don't, you won't help fight for Sophie?"

"I'm saying this ranch and the Knight name come first."

• • •

Becky laid Sophie back in her crib. She usually didn't wake up to eat at two a.m. anymore. Her pediatrician had said that was a sign she was ready for a little baby cereal.

Stretching her back, she headed for the kitchen to grab a bottle of water. In the hallway, she frowned at Logan's opened door. She glanced in his room. The covers were thrashed and he wasn't there.

Heaviness settled in her chest at the evidence of his nightmare. This time, she wouldn't leave him alone to suffer. She was his wife and she would damn well take care of him. Hooking the quilt with her fingers, she jerked it off the bed and went in search of her husband. Stepping out on the cold front porch, she called softly, "Logan?"

"Right here. Sophie okay?"

Wrapping the blanket around her shoulders, she walked across the deck. At least there was more moonlight tonight then the last time she'd discovered him out here. "You heard her cry? Did she wake you?" He wore only his black pajama bottoms. His eyes were smudged with fatigue and something much darker. Memories?

"Her cries rescued me from my nightmare. And you…" He closed his eyes and his hands fisted on the arms of the chair. "Go inside. Close your door. Tell me to stay out."

So much raw need crackled in his voice, her skin tingled. He held himself back, separate and alone. The air between them vibrated with a magnetic force tugging them close.

For a week they'd both resisted.

No more. She let the blanket slide off. Pressing her hands on his shoulders, she said softly, "No. I don't want you to stay out. I want you buried so deep inside me, I'll carry the memory of you and our time together until my last breath."

Saying the truth and accepting it freed her. She wanted Logan with no conditions, no lines. That wasn't bad, it was real and honest. They weren't making promises.

They were making memories.

She wanted them. She might never find this again, a man who saw her like he did.

His nostrils flared, his arms bulged. Then something snapped and Logan surged up out of the chair.

Becky stumbled back, tangling in the blanket.

His hands closed around her waist, catching her. "I won't let you fall." Leaving one hand on her, he scooped the blanket off the ground, swung it around her shoulders, and pulled her to his mouth. "Open, sugar."

She tilted her face up and kissed him. God, he tasted good, like a rich wine sliding over her tongue and creating hunger for more. Decadent and enticing, she chased his tongue, catching and sucking until he groaned.

Logan shifted, pulling back enough to lightly sink his teeth in her bottom lip, then licking the slight sting, creating tingles down her throat. Her breasts grew heavy, her nipples sensitive against his chest.

She ran her palms down his sides, desperate to memorize his powerful body. Loving the feel of his muscles bunching and shifting beneath her touch, she couldn't get enough of him.

He pressed his erection against her belly. Breaking the kiss, he buried his face in her hair. "Becky, I want you."

She dragged her hands around to caress his warm skin, then over the waistband of his cotton pants. His muscles twitched, showing her how much power a small touch had over this huge man. "You have me."

Cupping her face, his eyes burned into hers. "I don't have a condom out here, but I can make you come. No one is here. It's just us under the moonlight. Will you let me do that?"

"No."

He went completely still. It was long seconds before he said, "Not outside?"

"It's my turn. I want to see you in the moonlight." Dipping her thumbs into his pants, she kissed his jaw, his stubble rough on her lips. She loved the feeling of Logan like this—raw and real. Unable to resist, she licked the sexy dip between his throat and shoulder.

Logan shivered, his fingers digging into her hair and sliding over her scalp. "Take what you want."

She tracked down the path of his muscles, finding every groove. Lifting her head, she said, "I've wanted to do this since that first night when you came out of the shower and posed. You had these tiny beads of water sliding down and disappearing beneath the towel." She tugged his pants down an inch. Then stopped.

"Where did you see the water go?" Desire thickened his voice.

"Here." She flicked her tongue around a nipple, then licked the tip.

His hand tightened in her hair, creating a sensual sting on her scalp. "And?"

"Down here." After dragging her tongue over his ribs, she added, "And then all these ridges here." Becky crouched lower, her thighs protesting after all her time spent in the saddle today. She didn't care, her entire focus was on Logan. The way his muscles clenched at the touch of her mouth, his breath hissing when she licked the inside of his hipbone.

It wasn't enough. Sitting back on her heels, she slowly drew his pants down his legs.

His cock sprang free, erect and proud. Wrapping her hand around the base, she stroked up the silken steel. He was long and thick, and when she reached the head, she brushed the pad of her thumb over the swollen tip.

"You keep touching me, I won't last." He pushed into her hand.

She tilted her head up. Dusky color rode his cheekbones, his eyes burned. "Then how about I lick you instead?"

Before he could answer, Becky drew her tongue slowly up his length then closed her mouth around him.

• • •

Logan's chest locked as her mouth glided along his shaft. Like paradise. He struggled to keep control, but then he looked down.

The thin moonlight spilled over her tangled honey hair, her eyes closed as his swollen cock tunneled into her hot mouth. The blanket had slid from her shoulders, leaving her in a raspberry-colored tank and white panties kneeling at his feet. So damned giving. Filling all the ugly cracks inside of him with her sweet beauty.

In two months or so, she would be gone.

A primitive drive exploded in him. He had to possess her, get so deep inside her, she'd never be free of him. Never. He reached down, pulled her up to his mouth. Jerking the blanket from the ground, he tossed it over the railing and sat her on it.

"I—"

"You want me so deep inside you, you won't forget me. That's what you said."

"Yes."

Logan shoved up her shirt until her breasts spilled out. "Hold onto my shoulders." Bracing one hand on her lower back to hold her, he cupped her breast and dragged his tongue over the distended nipple. Her answering shudder goaded him into lightly scraping his teeth over the sensitive bud. A breathy moan rewarded him.

Her fingers dug into his shoulder, her hips moving. "It's not enough. Please."

Her desperate cry arrowed through him. Lifting his head, he saw it there in her, too. So little time. How would they get enough? His cock throbbed to get inside her. "You need this." He drew his hands up her bare thighs, feeling goosebumps rise on her skin. Pressed her legs apart. "Say it." He needed to know he wasn't alone, wasn't using her.

"I need us. For however long we have."

That shredded the last of his control. Logan shoved aside her panties and cupped his hand over her. Oh hell. She was slick and wet, her folds swollen. When he circled her clit, she whimpered. "Don't walk away. Don't leave me like this."

Shame and fury at himself rivaled the fierce lust and huge need for her. He'd walked away from her that night a week ago, humiliating her. "Never again, baby. You need my arms, my mouth, or my cock, and they're yours." With both hands he gripped the damp panel of material nestled between her thighs, and ripped it.

Grabbing hold of his shaft, he lined up to her entrance. The silky wet sensation nearly made his eyes roll back. So damn good. Couldn't stop. He powered into her.

Becky gasped, her eyes wide and vulnerable. "Condom."

Sheathed in her body, he tried to think. But he was lost. Becky surrounded him, he was feeling every part of her with nothing between them. "I don't want a barrier. No more barriers."

She wrapped her long legs around him, her soft thighs cradling his hips and Logan's mind blazed hot. He jerked her forward, thrusting balls-deep. Pulled out.

Again.

Nothing felt like this. So damned perfect as her body closed around him, her walls gloving him. Logan sealed his mouth over hers, tasting her cries as he pumped, finding every spot that made her moan, gasp, bite his tongue, and beg.

Fire raced down his spine. His balls drew up. His heart thundered as everything slid away but them. Becky in his arms, her mouth on his, her legs around him as he surged into her molten channel.

Her legs trembled. Walls tightened. His cock swelled, going impossibly hard. Breaking the kiss, he locked into her gaze. Clamping her hip, he tilted her until he was rubbing over her clit with every thrust.

Becky threw her head back and convulsed. Hard. Her entire body shaking. Raw, greedy cries spilling from her throat.

He slammed into her and exploded. Burying his face in her neck, he inhaled her honeysuckle scent. This moment was so perfect he didn't want to let it go. He should be worried, afraid, or, at the very least, anxious about not using a condom. But Becky's hands on him chased everything away except the need to care for her. He pulled back to see her soft eyes. "Sleep with me. Please." He could do it if she let him hold her.

"Okay. Here or in your bed?"

He closed his eyes, swallowing that thick knot in this throat. Not the usual rage that choked him, but something much bigger, more frightening in its own way.

The hope of Becky.

She'd come to him, given him her body with no barriers, and now she was willing to sleep out here on the porch if that was what he needed. Except she wouldn't sleep. Oh no, not his girl, she loved her baby too much and would go in the house every twenty minutes to check her child. Logan pulled up his pants, handed her shirt to her, then gathered her in his arms. "I want my wife in my bed."

But for how long?

Did he have it in him to be more than a temporary husband?

Chapter Thirteen

Wet licks on his hand woke Logan. Jiggy had his paws on the edge of the bed and lapped away at his fingers. Sun streamed in his windows, surprising him. Scratching the dog's head to distract him, he glanced at the clock.

Seven a.m. He'd slept for more than three hours and later than usual.

Becky burrowed into his side, bringing back the memory of the night. He stroked her hair, his chest warming at the memories. She was the reason he'd slept. Something about feeling her alive and breathing in his arms relaxed him, held the nightmares back.

Soft, pitiful cries pierced his thoughts.

Sophie. That's why Jiggy had woke him—he'd seen the dog let Becky know when the baby woke from her nap before. Now he'd have to get Becky up.

You could get Sophie for her. Try it. You've been able to hold her while riding.

But that was outside. His claustrophobia didn't kick in outside.

The baby's cries pitched up and Becky frowned in her sleep. Damn, she was tired. Okay, he eased his arm out from under her, slipped from the bed, and headed into the other room.

Sophie twisted on her back, her little face scrunched up, hands fisted. She drew her knees up then kicked straight out.

Pick her up. Just take her to her mom.

But she's so little. So fragile. The room heated. Buzzing started in his ears, and air thickened. Made it hard to breathe.

He needed air.

"Logan." Becky laid her hand on his back. "I've got her. Go shower or get some coffee."

Damn, he hadn't heard her come in.

Becky took her hand away to reach for the baby.

Coward. She's just a baby, an innocent child. "Wait."

She froze leaning halfway into the crib. Sophie had gone quiet at their voices, her huge eyes watching them both.

Logan unclenched his hands and softened his voice. "I want to pick her up. I have to be able to do this."

Her eyes melted into tenderness. "Are you sure?"

He dragged in the heavy air, forcing himself to keep breathing. "Yes."

Becky pulled back.

Logan rubbed his sweaty hands on his pants. It was ridiculous, he could handle a terrified horse that had been abused and teach the creature to trust him. He'd pulled injured friends from enemy fire, rescued captured Marines and protected civilians.

Becky's hand settled on his back. "I could pick her up

and hand her to you."

There was zero judgment in her eyes or voice. Just warm support as she tried to make this easier for him. "I should be able to do this. She's just a baby." Frustration clawed at him.

"When Sophie was born, they put her in my arms, and I was overwhelmed with love and fear. Here was this tiny little human, so perfect and totally, 100 percent relying on me for everything. Once we were home, I was so tired. But when I fell asleep, I had these awful dreams where I would take Sophie some place and forget her. I'd wake up in total terror, my heart pounding, couldn't breathe. I'd leap out of bed and check her basinet."

Logan leaned his forehead against hers.

"I sound stupid, don't I? Thinking my little story somehow compares to what you've been though. I'm sorry."

"No." His throat was raw. "You are so much more than beautiful. So much. You make me feel sane." How long had it been since he hadn't felt broken and unworthy?

"You are sane. Insane is screaming, jumping around, and running like a lunatic from bees. That just stirs them up. You're dealing with your issues. You got help. I hid from mine because I hated remembering that I'm allergic. So irrational. I didn't cause my father and brother to die by getting stung and having an allergic reaction, but my brain won't get the message. My response is crazy."

He wrapped his arms around her. Everything in him wanted to protect Becky from ever experiencing pain like that. And that meant he needed to hold Sophie with natural ease. The social worker would come to the house; he had to make this look real.

Sophie let out a bellow of impatience. Logan released

Becky and turned.

Don't think, just do it.

He leaned over, slipped his hands beneath her and lifted her up. She stopped bawling, but her lip quivered, and her wet eyes stared at him. A little shudder wracked her body.

Alive. She's alive. Safe.

He had her head in one hand and her butt and back in the other. "You want your mama, don't you?"

"Gah." She kicked his stomach.

"Why do I think you're saying 'Let's ride' rather than 'I'm hungry'?" Thinking of being on a horse with Sophie helped keep a lid on the bubbling anxiety hovering at the base of his spine. He turned, ready to hand her off.

Becky's fingers brushed his, creating a spark between them. She lifted her head, her eyes catching his and holding him while the baby was cradled between them. She felt it too—the connection growing and strengthening.

He wanted to kiss his wife. Hell, he wanted to give her more than just this pretend marriage. She'd come to him on the porch, let him take her the way he'd needed her freely, holding nothing back. And what did he do for her? He hadn't even taken her out, treated her the way a man should treat a woman.

Becky stroked his hand. "You can let go. I have her."

She wasn't getting it. "I thought I'd want to."

"You don't?"

"No." This moment stretched, wrapping around them, just Logan with his wife and step-baby.

"What's happening here?" She whispered it as if afraid to break the spell.

"You're turning me and my world inside out. You make

me want to be more than your temporary husband."

"Maybe it'd be better to stick to our agreement."

The hurt building in her eyes shamed him and he didn't know what the fuck to do. "I care about you. How about we take these next two months and see what happens? See if what we have is real and possible? No promises, no pressure." Yeah, way to woo her.

"Sure. We'll do that. No pressure."

"Let's go on a date tonight. Just casual, we'll go to Spinners, a friend of mine owns the bar. We'll dance, and if you ask real nice…maybe I'll show you my skills on the mechanical bull." He reconsidered as he heard it come out of his mouth. She deserved better than a sports bar. "Or I could take you to a nice dinner."

Her expression cleared as excitement filled her eyes. "I'd rather go to your friend's bar. It sounds like fun."

Better. This was better. "It's a date."

• • •

Becky's nerves danced and popped as they went into the bar. Logan had on dark jeans and a thin charcoal sweater pushed up to his elbows. He smelled awesome, soap and that richer male scent that was pure Logan.

A date. They were on a date.

Logan bent close to her ear. "That skirt you're wearing is distracting the hell out of me."

Her skin tingled. "That was the plan, cowboy."

"You're lucky I didn't ravish you in my truck."

"Hmm, not sure I would have objected."

Logan tugged her into his body, his eyes growing serious.

"Bad as I want you, when I make you come, it'll be in private."

Spinners was huge. Her gaze caught on the big mechanical bull surrounded by mats to the left of the door. It was currently roped off, a huge dude wearing chaps and a menacing expression deterring anyone who tried to breech the barrier. She took in the rustic wood beamed ceilings, plank floors, and a gleaming bar on the right. For a Sunday night, the place was pretty full.

"Logan!" A voice boomed through the room. A large man strode up to them.

"Mac." Logan did the hand shake, half hug thing. "How you been?"

"Can't complain. Now who is this beauty?" His dark eyes landed on her.

"This is Becky, my wife."

Mac's craggy face blanked for a second. "You son of a gun, you're married? To this lovely woman?"

"Yep."

Becky held out her hand. "Nice to meet you, Mac."

"Huh." The older man ignored her hand and engulfed her in a bear hug. Setting her down, he grinned. "How'd Logan lasso a pretty little thing like you?"

She laid her hand on the man's arm. "Actually, I lassoed him. He never saw it coming."

Mac threw his head back and laughed. Wiping his eyes, he slapped Logan's shoulder. "You've done good. Come on, let's get you two some drinks."

Mac waved off the bartenders as Becky slipped onto a barstool. Logan stood by her, his arm draped across the back of her stool. "Mac, Logan tells me that you own the bar. It's nice."

"Sure do. Bought it after I stopped bull riding." He set a glass of white wine in front of Becky and handed Logan a beer.

She sipped her wine, enjoying the chance to let loose a little since Pam was giving Sophie a bottle tonight. "So that mechanical bull over there in the corner? Is that just for show?"

The older man grinned. "You want to ride it?"

In this skirt? Becky didn't think so. "Another time. But Logan's been bragging to me that he can stay on it."

Logan's head snapped around. "Are you doubting me, sugar?"

"Just saying that I think a man ought to be able to back up his words. Am I right, Mac?"

Mac's booming laughter filled the bar. "Son, you got yourself a whole heap of trouble in this one."

Logan's eyes gleamed "Why don't you warm up that bull." He took Becky's hand. "I'm going to see if I can wear my wife out a little on the dance floor."

"Ha." One sip of wine and Becky was feeling feisty. "What do you suppose my talent was in pageants?"

"Looking hot?"

She rolled her eyes. "Dance. I took years of dance classes. I was good enough that I almost won a trip to see the San Francisco Ballet in one of my pageants. I planned to take my mom, but, unfortunately, Ava beat me that day and I came in second." A poignant memory washed over her. "Mom and I talked about saving up and going when she got well. We spent hours dreaming about it, looking at websites and planning…" Trailing off, she realized Logan had stopped halfway to the dance floor.

His eyes softened. "You can go in memory of your mom. You'll have the money."

She didn't want to talk about the money, the contract, or her mom. Not now when she was on a date. Tonight she wanted to dance, laugh, and make Logan want her. Crave her as much as she craved him. Shrugging off the memory, she raised her eyebrows. "Are you trying to get out of dancing with me? Afraid you can't keep up?"

Heat leapt into his gaze. "Let's see your moves, pageant girl. Maybe you can win first place with me."

"Maybe?" Recalling the first time they kissed after she'd done her beauty pageant walk, she flash him her winning smile. "You don't have a prayer, cowboy." She tossed her hair and rolled her hips as she headed to the dance floor with his gaze searing her back.

Logan caught up to her, pulling her into his arms. "Swear to God, you walk like that again in that short skirt, and I'm going to drag you into Mac's office, lock the door, bend you over a table and rip your panties off. Again." He sucked in a breath. "Christ, I'm rock hard for you."

She'd made men want her before, but with Logan, it was different. He wanted her to sleep in his arms like she was special enough to be held and cherished. "Then what will you do? You know, once you rip my panties off?"

He narrowed his eyes, and his hand tightened on her lower back. Leaning to her ear, he growled, "First I'll slide my cock into you, slowly, letting you adjust. Letting you feel how hot and hard I am. Then you'll do that sexy little whimper and I'll know you want more."

She squeezed her thighs together. She'd meant to taunt him, but he was torturing her.

He groaned. "Don't lick your lips like that."

She hadn't even realized she'd done it. "What next?"

He stroked his hands to the curve of her hips. "I'll hold you like this from behind, and slam into you deep and fast until you come so hard, no other man will ever be enough for you. Only me."

Streaks of hot pleasure ripped through her. "Crap."

"What?"

"My panties are wet."

His eyes blazed with possessive heat. "Exactly how I like them."

• • •

For a week after her date night with Logan, Becky had tiny clues that he was up to something, but she'd never in a million years have guessed she'd find herself in a stunningly beautiful suite at the Fairmont Heritage Place in San Francisco. Peeling her gaze from the view of the bay, she said, "I can't believe you did this."

"There's more." Logan took her hand and led her past the sitting room to the bay view bedroom and retrieved the dress from the closet. "Pam said it would fit you."

Gasping, she fingered the beaded champagne colored cocktail dress. "Logan!" She'd been sewing pageant dresses since her teens and recognized quality, probably the creation of a high-end designer. She was too scared to look at the tags hanging from it. "It's exquisite." Snatching her hand back, she looked up into the proud glint in his light green eyes. "You did all this? The private plane, bringing me to San Francisco? The dress?" Everything had happened so quickly today, she still hadn't caught her breath.

"Pam and Pricilla helped me with all the arrangements, including getting the tickets."

Her heart stuttered. Anticipation and hope wound in her stomach. Pam had descended on her this morning, helping her and Sophie pack while refusing to tell her why. Her sister-in-law just kept insisting it was her job as *the nanny*. Then the limo, the plane ride, another limo….and now she was thrown another surprise. "What tickets?"

Returning the dress to the closet, Logan pulled her against him. Cupping her face, he said, "The ballet. It's Cinderella. I don't know shit about ballet, but that's seems fitting. For this weekend, I want to be your prince. I can't bring your mom back, but I can take you to the ballet the two of you dreamed of attending." He lifted her left hand and touched her mom's rings. "Tonight when we watch that ballet together, she'll be with you."

Her stomach bottomed out as her heart went into free fall—right into love with her husband, the man who surprised her with this extravagant trip just so she could feel close to her mom again. "Logan, thank you."

He smiled. "We'll have tonight together. After the ballet, a chef is cooking us dinner, and we'll eat on the balcony overlooking the bay."

It sounded perfect.

"In the morning, we'll take Sophie and the nanny—"

Laughter bubbled around the lump of pure happiness in her throat. "Quit calling your sister that." It touched her how much Pam was doing for her. She and Sophie had their own room and Pam seemed delighted to get so much time with the baby. Which reminded her. "Thank you for bringing

Sophie." It made her feel better, being near her daughter and able to feed or comfort her.

Fierceness weighed down his brows. "We're not leaving your daughter behind. She's a baby and needs you. Besides there's no way you'd have gotten on that plane without her. If we were staying close by, then maybe we could have snuck away for a night and left her in Pricilla and Pam's care."

Her heart just kept going in that free fall. It didn't even phase him to include Sophie. He held her more and more now, or laid on the floor, playing with her and Jiggy. But what really got her was that her baby's welfare was important to him.

"Anyway," he went on. "Tomorrow we'll take Sophie out to see the city before we fly home."

A riot of emotions erupted in her chest. Throwing her arms around his neck, she went up on her toes. "You're the best husband ever. I think you should win a prize."

His grin turned wicked. "Oh I will, sugar. I'm taking the prettiest woman out on the town, bringing her back here to feed her, and then I'm going to claim my prize." He slid his hand around her hip, his fingers clamping possessively. "Slowly, with careful attention to every bit of skin I reveal as I peel that dress off you."

Looking up into his light green eyes, Becky really did feel like Cinderella. For the moment, she had it all, everything she ever wanted.

Becky had a home and a family. She belonged.

But what would happen when the clock struck midnight or, in their case, the three months were up?

Chapter Fourteen

Becky couldn't tear her eyes from Pam as she raced her horse around the barrels. Sophie was so excited, Mac laughed. "Damn, girl, that baby loves the rodeo."

She didn't answer. Her heart was in her throat as Pam took her horse around another barrel at an angle that made Becky's lungs seize. Becky leaned as if she were on the horse, not her sister-in-law. "Go Pam!"

All of them were as close as they could get to watch Pam in her timed event. Brian, Pricilla, Abby, Logan's lawyer-friend Brody, and Mac all watched. More people came and went, many angling to get a chance to meet Becky.

Kendra hung out there, too.

Pam cleared the last barrel and road full bore to the finish line.

They all turned to the clock.

"First place!" Logan roared and turned. "Did you see that, Sophie? Your aunt took first place."

Sophie craned her head, trying to see Pam as she rode out of the ring. The baby's face crumpled and she protested when Pam was out of her sight.

"I'll be damned. She really did recognize her," Mac said.

Becky hugged her daughter, rocking and soothing her. "You can see Aunt Pammy soon." Her daughter adored Pam even more after their San Francisco trip.

"I got some great shots. Look at these, Logan." Kendra shoved her camera into his face.

Sophie sucked her fist, getting more agitated. "I'd better go feed her."

Logan looked over. "I'll walk with you."

"Hurry back, I have more shots I want to show you." Kendra patted Logan's arm.

Becky gritted her teeth and started walking, willing herself not to overreact. The last couple weeks with Logan had been amazing, and they spent each night wrapped in each other's arms. Today they were surrounded by family and friends enjoying the rodeo. But Kendra bugged Becky with her possessive tone around Logan and his family. And Logan…

We just fell into bed a couple times. Now it's over, it was nothing. His words haunted her—what if that's how Logan would feel about her at the end of three months?

He caught up to her. "Something bothering you?"

What did she say? She didn't own Logan, not really. Basically they had a three-month agreement. Yeah, things were going good, but Logan had said no promises.

"Talk to me, Becky."

"Kendra. She's always around." The thought of him touching Kendra, kissing her… Becky closed her eyes, struggling to swallow the vile emotion churning in her. She'd fallen deeply in love with her husband, but not knowing if he felt anything real for her brought out her vulnerabilities and jealousy.

"I've known her since I was eight. She's just a family friend."

"Who you had sex with." She winced, hearing her snappish tone. She didn't want to be that clinging, desperate girl who'd do anything for affection from a man.

"Are you jealous?" He tugged her to a stop and tucked a loose strand of hair back behind her ear. "I told you it was over. I don't hound you about men you had sex with." His eyes darkened. "I don't want to think about another man touching you."

"I haven't slept with anyone here, so you aren't running into them, imagining—"

"Shit, yeah that would piss me off." He put his arm around her shoulders, pulling her and Sophie into his side and resumed walking. "I get it, but I don't want to rock the boat too much. You saw the piece on you, me, and Sophie. She's showing us as a committed family, and that's good for both our goals."

"True. Even the social worker has seen it." They'd had a surprise visit from Molly Grover this week. She'd conducted their first interview for the court-ordered home study.

"Kendra knows we're over. I slept with her twice. I'd come home, she'd broken up with a boyfriend, and we used each other. That was it. I didn't feel anything for her, not like I feel for you."

Everything in her cried out for a commitment. Something more than *let's take two months and find out*. And, *no promises, no pressure.* They reached the area where the Knights had parked their trailer. "I'm fine. I'll feed Sophie and if she sleeps, I'll rest in here, too. Go on, go hang out with Brody and Mac."

"But not Kendra. You're the woman I want." He kissed her then strode off.

Becky went into the front half of the trailer that was as nice as any motor home. The back portion housed the horses and tack. She quickly changed Sophie and settled her into breastfeeding. They had both dozed off when she heard a commotion.

"Let me go."

She snapped awake, recognizing Pam's voice. After quickly fixing her shirt, she laid Sophie in the travel crib.

"Cade, stop it. I'm not in the mood."

"Well I am."

Chills went down her spine at the man's ugly tone. Becky opened the door, went out, and looked around.

"No." Pam's upset voice came from the horse trailer.

Becky strode around to the opened back end. Inside, the man had Pam pinned to the wall. "You couldn't get your mouth on my dick fast enough last time. You want it, all whores want it." He shoved his mouth on Pam's while his hand went to his belt buckle.

Whore. That word exploded in Becky's head. She stormed into the trailer and grabbed a broom from the wall mount. "Let her go!" She wacked the broom against the bastard's back.

Cade yelped and spun around. He was about even with Becky in height, but he had more meat on him and his face turned purple with fury.

Pam ran past Becky.

"Bitch, you'll pay for that. You want to play with a broom?" He advanced on her.

Shit. Sophie was alone in the other part of the trailer. She turned to tell Pam to get the baby away from here, but the girl was gone.

A wall of pissed off male slammed into her. Becky hit the floor of the trailer. She felt a shock of hot pain in her left forearm. Dang, that hurt. She tried to roll off her arm, but she was trapped by the heavy weight. "Get off."

Becky fought, her muscles straining but he had her pinned. Sick fear spread through her.

A roar sounded, and Becky lifted her head as Logan exploded into the trailer. He picked up the man as if he weighed nothing and threw him clean out of the trailer.

Logan leaped out after him.

"Becky, oh God." Pam knelt by her, crying. A blur of people filled the trailer.

My baby is alone in the trailer. Have to make sure she's safe.

Worry for her baby drove out any thoughts of pain. Rolling over, she blurted out, "Sophie's in the living quarters."

Pricilla whipped off her jacket and wrapped Becky's arm. "I'll go get her, but honey, don't move for a few minutes. Your arm's bleeding, and we need to make sure you're okay. " She got up and said, "Abby, take a look at Becky, see if we need the EMTs."

Becky couldn't lay there on the trailer floor, so she carefully sat up. Heat prickles broke out on her body, black spots danced in front of her eyes for a few seconds.

"Breathe, Becky," Abby knelt next to her and Pam. "Did you hit your head?" She unwrapped her arm, examining it.

"No. Just my knees and arm." Taking a couple breaths, the pain in her arm eased and everything slid into focus. It was just shock, she wasn't really hurt. Outside the trailer, Cade was crumpled and moaning on the ground. Logan stood over him, every muscles and tendon bulging.

"What the hell happened?" Brian bellowed.

"It's my fault," Pam burst out, her eyes wet with tears.

Her father turned on her. "What did you do?"

Pam gestured to Cade writhing on the ground. "He attacked me. I went home with him the other night—"

Brian's face turned purple. "When you act like a whore this is what happens! First you got thrown out of college and now this."

"Brian!" Priscilla stopped at the edge of the trailer, her lips white. "What is wrong with you? That's our daughter and she's just been attacked." The woman was so angry, her voice shook. Charging into the trailer, she handed Sophie to Becky and hugged Pam.

Her aunt's sobs caused the baby to wail in distress.

Becky held her daughter to her chest, and tried to keep from crying, too. How could this happen? Pam had been attacked and now Brian was calling his daughter something so awful.

• • •

Logan leaned against the trailer that housed the first aid station for the rodeo. He still couldn't believe Becky hit Cade with a broom to protect Pam. She should have come to him, or called him on his cell. That guy could have killed her. When he'd run up and saw Cade on top of Becky, heard her cry out, he'd gone right into kill mode. It'd taken Brody and Mac to pull him off the man.

All he wanted to do now was scoop up his wife and stepdaughter and take them home. Pricilla was having none of that—she was mothering Becky by cleaning and bandaging the cut on her arm. Logan had been firmly kicked out of the first aid station. Pam and Sophie were with them, too.

His father strode up and Logan shoved off the trailer to confront Brian. "What the hell was that, calling Pammy a whore?" His sister's ravaged face twisted his guts. He wanted better than an animal like Cade for his sister, but she wasn't a whore. She was a sweet, beautiful girl who loved animals, clothes, and, judging by how she adored Sophie, babies. She just didn't know what she wanted to do with her life yet, and last time Logan checked, that was part of growing up.

His father glanced at the trailer then back at him. "I won't have my daughter running around with lowlifes. She's not going to end up like your mother, singing in dive bars, sleeping on buses and chasing tail."

Logan wasn't even shocked. Nothing changed. Somehow, someway, his father always brought everything back to his mother. Always.

"Nor will I have my son making a fool out of our family name." Brian ran his hand through his hair. "All this psychobabble about a bullshit camp with a bunch of long-haired hippies crying because they had to do a man's job. It makes me want to puke."

Logan refused to rise to the bait. The entire battle

between him and Brian was wearing on him. "Do you have a point? Because I have a wife to take care of."

"A wife who had another man's kid four months ago."

It took every technique he'd learned to keep his temper. "Be very careful how you talk about my wife. Becky's better than all of us. In case you didn't notice, she saved Pammy's ass tonight."

"Yeah, she's got mettle, I'll give her that. Now it's time you prove your manhood. No more chasing after your dreams like your hippie mother."

"You mean the woman you were in love with and married?" Hmm, guess he was rising to the bait after all. Would he and his father ever break out of this same old routine?

"Fine, I loved her. But you know what? She wanted me to choose between her and the ranch. She ran off and I chose to be a man and do my duty. I learned my lesson. Love means nothing. I found a decent woman, married her, and made it work. Love has nothing to do with it."

The gasp in the doorway caused both men to spin.

Pricilla stood with Becky, Sophie, and Pam. His stepmom stomped down the steps and slapped her hands on her hips. "You never loved me? All these years, I gave you two kids, took in your son from another woman as my own, and you don't love me?" Hurt and anger colored her face and vibrated in her voice.

Logan couldn't believe how the family was unraveling. Scaling the steps, he took Sophie from his sister, kissed her cheek, then helped Becky down. "Come on, I'm taking you and Sophie home."

Becky hesitated, her gaze sliding around the uneasy

group. "Uh, while we were in the first aid station, I told Pricilla and Pam they could stay at our house tonight. They don't want to go home with Brian after what he called Pam."

"No! Absolutely not." Brian bellowed. "My wife and daughter are coming home with me."

Pricilla got right up in his face. "Not until you apologize for calling Pam a whore. And even then, Brian…" Sadness dragged her shoulders down and softened her voice. "I don't know if I want to return to a man who doesn't love me."

Logan had no idea how all this had happened. Christ, he came home to his land for peace, not a family war.

Chapter Fifteen

Becky woke to her dog nuzzling her face. "Jiggy." The dog's sweet warmth cleared the nightmare she'd been having, but damn, she hurt all over from Cade tackling her. Logan had been right that she'd tighten up in the middle of the night. Turning her head, she saw the empty space next to her. "He's out on the porch, isn't he?"

Jiggy didn't answer.

She couldn't feel abandoned, though. Logan had taken care of her. He had brought her home, settled Pricilla and Pam, and then Logan had taken her in the hot bath. He just held her there, letting the water ease her sore muscles. After that, he'd tucked her into bed and held her until she'd slept.

Forcing herself to her feet, she took the two Advil waiting for her. Becky wrapped a blanket around herself then stopped at the door to her baby's room. She eased it open. Pam and Pricilla slept on the bed and Sophie slept in her crib.

Jiggy went to the dog bed beneath Sophie's crib.

Becky left the door ajar and headed out to the porch.

"Becky?" Logan cut her off before she got two steps outside. "What do you need?"

The moonlight spilled over him, illuminating his stark bones and empty eyes. She hated his torment. "Just you."

He glanced at the door, his jaw clamping with iron determination. "All right, let's go to bed."

She touched his face. "You'd do it, wouldn't you?"

"What?" His gaze stayed locked on that door.

"Force yourself through the door. For me."

"It's okay, I can do it."

She believed he could. That he'd done it many times before and no one noticed. He'd learned to cope with his symptoms and find a way to live, but not to heal his heart. "I don't want to go inside. I just want your arms around me."

Finally, he dragged his gaze to hers. "It's cold. You'll be more comfortable in bed."

She shook her head, then winced at a stab of pain. "Not if you're suffering. Please, Logan, let me stay out here with you. I already took the Advil you left for me, I just…you said if I ever needed you to hold me, you would. I need that." She hadn't meant to beg him, but it was the truth.

His jaw softened. "I'll hold you." He led her to the chair, sat, and eased her onto his lap so she rested against his steady heartbeat.

The nightmare weighed on her, and she blurted out, "Dylan called me a whore when I told him I was pregnant. He said I tried to trap him. So did his parents. In the hallway of the courthouse, they screamed at me that I was a gold-digging whore."

His muscles flexed and swelled. "You're not a whore."

"I know that logically, but words have a strange power. They dig in deep, burrow where we can't see them and release a slow poison that taints our lives." She took a breath and added, "Like our first kiss. It was wonderful, the best kiss I'd ever experienced, but when I realized I was losing control, Dylan and his parents' words echoed in my head."

He leaned his face to hers. "There was nothing wrong about that, baby. Nothing. All I saw and felt was a beautiful, sweet woman trusting me enough to give her pleasure." He kissed her hair. "You never hold back with me now, do you?"

How could she not have fallen in love with him? "No. When you touch me, I feel safe, sexy, and whole." Like right now in his arms. Before she lost her train of thought, she went on, "Logan, that man and your father called Pam a whore. That's going to sink deep and fester. She needs you to help her excise that."

He recoiled. "Me?"

"You're her big brother. She's adored you forever. Promise me you'll talk to her. Don't let that word burrow too deep inside your sister's heart."

Logan eyes softened. "I'll talk to her."

"Good." She rested her head on his chest.

He stroked her hair. "Did you come out here because you were worrying about Pam?"

"I woke, you were gone and…" What did she tell him? "I missed you. I guess having me in bed with you doesn't ease your nightmares anymore." Logan had told her that he had fewer nightmares when she slept with him, and if he did have one, having her close enough to pull her into his arms calmed him.

Logan stared into her eyes. "That's not it. I—shit." He rubbed his hand over his face.

"What? You can tell me."

"Every time I went to sleep, I was right back in Afghanistan in a remote village, reliving the moment when I forced myself to go through the door of a tiny mud house, even though black dread filled every goddamned cell in my body. But I had a job to do, so I did it. I went through that door."

Becky sucked in her breath.

"Only this time in my nightmare, it wasn't eight young girls, a man, his wife, and a tiny baby that I found dead. It was you and Sophie dead. I got there too late."

He'd suffered something awful beyond her ability to truly understand. "They were murdered?"

"The family was running an underground school for girls. The Taliban killed them all, even the baby."

That was why he came outside and had to sometimes force himself to go through a door.

"They were dead.." He looked into her eyes. "I snapped that day. I'd heard the term red rage before, but the moment I saw that dead baby, that's exactly what filled my mind. Hunt and I—"

"Who is Hunt?"

"Another Marine, Hunter Reece. He works for Once a Marine, too. We quickly picked up the trail of those baby killers and...ended them. Some of it I don't remember, or maybe I just don't want to remember it."

She shivered at the utter ice in him. He was retreating, pulling back inside himself and could she blame him? God, what he'd seen. And what he'd probably done to the killers in his rage…that couldn't be an easy thing to remember. She stayed quiet, unsure if he realized how much he'd told her. Instead, she pressed her palm against his, and laced their fingers together.

"It was worse in the nightmare tonight, seeing yours and Sophie's faces like that." He rubbed his thumb over her hand. "I jerked awake and needed you so damned bad I broke into a sweat trying to keep from touching you."

"You've pulled me into your arms other nights, so why not tonight?" She couldn't change what he'd lived through, but she could keep him from being alone when he hurt because of it now.

"You're sore and need your rest. I didn't want to wake you." He pulled his fingers from hers, tried to press her head down. "I won't use you like that."

But he would make himself go through the door for her, even when it caused him anxiety? He'd come to her rescue without a second's hesitation at the rodeo. But she couldn't comfort him when he needed care? Fierce emotion boiled in her. Logan had been alone too long. No one had fought for him, no one had held him. Yet he'd been strong and smart enough to find a therapist to help him cope with the PTSD, and now he was building a camp to reach other veterans who'd felt as alone as he had.

And he was still alone with no one to help him heal his heart. Until now.

"You don't get to do that. You don't."

Startled, he pulled his head back. "Do what?"

"Hold back when you need me. Earlier you said I don't hold back with you anymore. But you should have woken me, told me you needed me."

His eyes caught the moonlight and glittered. "And then what, Becky? Tell you to spread your legs because I needed you so bad I felt like I was dying? That I needed to prove we're both still alive? That I need to be so deep inside your body I could feel your heart beating? Ask that of you when you just got knocked around by a bastard, because I wasn't there to protect you? Is that what you're telling me I should have done?"

She glared at him. "Yes."

The sharp lines of his face throbbing with anger melted into utter confusion. "You can't be serious."

"I am. You wouldn't hurt me. You'd be gentle because I'd need that right now and together we would find comfort and pleasure. I know this because you are the man I not only trust with my heart and body—"

Fear rode into his eyes and set up camp, leeching away the beautiful green and leaving behind a sickly shade.

She refused to back down. He needed to know that she cared. "You are the man I love. I didn't know what real love for a man was until you."

He sucked in a tortured breath, then shook his head, trying to deny her words.

Catching hold of his face, she knew Logan would look at her, because he was too strong a man, too honorable to do anything else. This was the man who didn't want to go through the door that hellish day so long ago in Afghanistan, but he'd done that, too.

With her eyes locked on his, she told him her absolute truth. "I love you."

His warm hand covered hers, while his gaze undulated with regret. "People don't love me. Not like that."

He believed that, and her throat ached. "I do." Before he could object, or try to sooth her feelings, she added softly, "I'm here for you as long as you want me."

• • •

Want her?

He didn't think he could breathe without her and that terrified him.

God, she gave him everything. Logan hadn't ever had this. Was it real? Could he trust it? A part of him held back.

A part of him *always* held back.

While Becky exposed her heart and offered him her body.

Rising, he carried her to his room, eased the door closed, and settled her on the sheets. The moonlight streamed in, showing him his beautiful girl. Her honey blond hair spread around her face, brown eyes on him.

Only him.

With her good arm, she reached to shove her panties down.

He caught her hand, his chest inflating at her love. "No." His cock disagreed, but the rest of Logan meant it. "You're what I need. Sex will wait until you're feeling better." Easing onto the bed, he turned her to her side and put a pillow beneath her injured arm. The cut wasn't that bad, but Logan needed to take care of her. It felt...right.

"I want to. I love it when you're inside me."

She was going to kill him saying things like that. His cock twitched hard against her soft bottom, but he wasn't taking any chances that could hurt her. All he needed was this—his wife in his arms. He wanted to share a part of him with her. "Becky."

"Hmm?"

She was going soft and fluid. The Advil was working and exhaustion was pulling her under. Would she remember what he told her? "After I came to live at the ranch, I didn't fit anywhere. Didn't belong. I knew that this spot of land would be mine one day so I came here to escape. In those days, I had a little fort I built where the house is now."

"I wish I'd seen it, a special place that was all yours. That's why this land is so important to you, and why it's been your touchstone when the PTSD rears up. It's your safe place."

She always did that, heard what he said and understood it as best as another person could. Made him feel seen and heard. Worthy. He slipped his hand beneath her tank to her belly. That connection with her soothed the ragged edge of his memories. "Yes."

"Did you ever visit your mom?"

Barren emptiness opened in his chest. "The custody agreement required she visit me on the ranch. She couldn't take me anywhere. She came a few times, but she left. Usually when I was asleep." He'd wake and she'd be gone again.

Becky twisted her head, her eyes on him. "That's cruel."

Here it was, the truth he'd never said out loud. "I learned to stop needing anyone. It was easier. Alone is easier." He was trying to give Becky a reason not to walk away when the contract ended.

Tell her you care, that what you're feeling for her must be love.

But he couldn't. "I'm trying to change, to learn how to be with you."

She turned away, settling into sleep, while Logan hated himself for holding back. Deep down, he couldn't help but admit the truth to himself. His mother hadn't been able to commit—not to her husband or her son.

Was he just like her?

• • •

Becky opened the door and barely repressed a groan. "Kendra." Fifth time in the last ten days the woman had dropped by. She was on Becky's last nerve. "What's up?"

Without waiting for an invitation, the other woman walked in. "I've brought by a few things from the house for Pricilla." Kendra went to the table and held out a bag. "Brian really wants you to come home. He's misses you."

Resigned, Becky dropped into a chair by Pricilla. Kendra was working closely with Brian on photographing the ranch for new shots on the Knight Ranch website. And somehow, she'd ended up being Brian's messenger girl, too.

Probably because Abby refused to get involved. From what Becky heard, she had told her father that he was wrong and it was his job to man up and apologize. Brian, evidently, didn't like that advice. Which meant Becky got a steady dose of Kendra in her home.

But just because Kendra irritated Becky like a rash, didn't mean she was wrong. "Maybe you should talk to him." Her mother-in-law had dug in, not budging. So far, the standoff had lasted ten days. Pricilla had even cancelled the barbeque, which was telling. That woman loved a party. But the family was too fractured to even pretend unity.

Pricilla shook her head. "He wants to talk to me, he can

come over here. Pam and I are waiting for an apology."

Kendra shot a helpless gaze at Becky. "This can't go on. Aren't you guys cramped living in this house?"

"We manage." She didn't mind; she'd loved the family feeling and Sophie was thriving. They'd moved the double bed into the third bedroom that used to be Logan's office.

Pricilla smiled at Becky then said, "Kendra, I know you're trying to help, but this is between me and my husband."

Kendra sighed. "You're right. That's exactly what I told Brian, but he keeps finding reasons to send me over here and try to talk to you and Pam into coming home." She shook her head. "My dad's the same way. Their pride prevents them from saying sorry, you know?"

"I've always made the first move and gone the extra mile, but he crossed the line saying Pam acted like a whore. If I don't stand up for my daughter now, then I'd hate myself forever." Pricilla stirred her cup of coffee.

Becky was trying to think of the least offensive way to tell Kendra it was time to go when the front door opened, spilling in Logan and a bubbling Pam. "Mom, you have to see the new horse! She's gorgeous. Logan and I worked with… Oh, hi Kendra."

Logan put his hands on Becky's shoulders. "After we get your allergy shot today, you can ride her if you like. She's gentle."

"You'll love her, Becky." Pam practically danced.

Becky couldn't help but smile. Logan was taking Pam with him to work on his camp and Pam absorbed the attention. "I can't wait."

"Come on, Becky, we need to get to your appointment." Logan leaned down to the baby. "Are you coming with us, half pint?"

Sophie held out her arms.

Logan laughed and lifted her high over his head, making her giggle.

"You won't be laughing when she throws up on you," Becky said as she grabbed her purse and the diaper bag. "We'll walk you out, Kendra."

"I'm going to stay a few more minutes."

She hesitated, trying to think of a polite way to tell her to get out and leave them alone.

"It's fine, let's go." Logan held the door for Becky.

Once they were in the truck, she blurted, "Don't you think it's odd that Kendra is so involved in this fight between your dad and Pricilla?"

He glanced over, surprise etching into his face. "You're mad?"

"Not mad. Just tired of her being underfoot. She makes me uneasy. Kendra didn't need to stay there when we left." Becky had been trying to steer her out. "It's not her family."

"She's there for Pricilla, not me. Don't let her get to you."

Frustrated, she shut up, but all she could think about was that Logan's birthday was just weeks away—the deadline on their marriage. Would Logan want Becky and Sophie to stay?

He took her hand. "Let's take advantage of our live-in babysitters and go out tonight."

He was changing the subject, but they could both use a night out. "Sure, where?"

"I rented a suite at a hotel. How does room service and champagne in a hot tub sound?"

"You already planned it?" Hope surged in her; this

wasn't just to appease her. Maybe he wanted to talk about their future.

"Oh, I have plans…" Logan shot her a sinful grin. "…to keep you naked, well fed, and sexually satisfied until we are forced to return to my house crammed full of people."

"Will you be naked, too?"

"And hard."

She lifted her chin. "A naked and hard cowboy, hmm, that has real possibilities."

Logan's phone rang. He glanced at the number, then he answered it through the truck's Bluetooth. "Adam, what's up?"

A deep voice replied. "I need you in Houston. A laboratory there had a security breech, we've been hired to find it and you're closest."

"I'm on leave."

The man drew a deep breath. "We're all putting in twelve-hour days. This is a quick job, twenty-four to thirty-six hours max."

Logan looked over at her. "I'm sort of involved in something."

"Aside from the camp?" Adam's voice lost the irritated distraction.

"Yes."

Her stomach plunged as she realized he wasn't going to tell Adam about her. Why? Was she some kind of dirty little secret?

"Is it so important that you can't get away for a day or two?"

Logan's hesitation filled the cab.

Becky put her hand on his arm. "Go," she mouthed.

"I'll do it. Send the intel. I'll go over it when I get home."

"Sienna has booked your flight, you leave tonight." The call disconnected.

"That was your boss?" She stared out the windshield as Logan pulled in and parked in front of the medical building.

"Yes, Adam Waters. Sienna Lorrey is his administrative assistant."

"They don't know we're married?"

He looked over at her. "Not their business."

"But they know about the camp."

He frowned at her. "Yes. That's not the same thing. Look, if you don't want me to go, I'll call him back."

The camp was his true passion and he'd been straight up honest with her about it. "No, it's fine." Her insecurity was dragging her right back into being the woman she didn't want to be. She couldn't make Logan love her and want to tell people about her. Or support her when she wanted Kendra out of her house. She reached for the door.

Logan caught her hand. "While I'm gone, stay close to home. Dylan's still out there."

"He hasn't done anything since the tire incident." Focusing on that was easier than thinking about their relationship. "Once he found out I was married to you, he backed off."

"Don't take chances." His eyes softened. "I'm sorry about tonight. I really wanted to spend time alone with you. We'll do it when I get back."

Chapter Sixteen

"You look like you can use this." Pricilla poured a cup of coffee and slid it across the bar.

Becky settled on the barstool. "Thanks." Sophie was leaning over Becky's arm, swinging her arms at Jiggy and chattering away.

"Looks like you didn't sleep much. Missing Logan?"

All she'd thought about was what it would be like if she had to get used to being alone again. "Yeah, guess I'm not used to sleeping alone anymore."

"Sucks, doesn't it? But at least yours is coming back tomorrow."

Forgetting her own worries, she eyed her mother-in-law. "How are you doing?"

She shrugged. "I'm living in a state of disbelief. All these years, I stuck it out because I thought he loved me. Oh, he didn't say it, but I guess I wanted to believe it. Hearing him tell Logan he never loved me snapped me out of that fantasy. But what he said to Pam…I hope Brian apologizes. He might not love me, but his daughter loves him and needs her father." Pricilla sipped some coffee, then leaned on her forearms. "On the upside, Pam and I are getting closer to Logan by staying here. Before he married you, living together like this would never have happened, he'd stay somewhere else. He's changing, letting us in more. You're good for him."

She wasn't sure what to say to that. But she was curious. "Did you know he had PTSD?"

"Not for a while. About six months ago he came home and showed us the plans for his camp. That's when I realized what Logan had been enduring, but Brian lost his temper. It was ugly."

"Why?"

"He was raised in a different generation by a miserable old bastard who ruled with an iron fist. He tolerated no weakness, no hint of softness in his son. Brian broke free once with Indigo. Stood up to the old man, married her, and brought her to the ranch. Then she ran…and the old man never let him forget his mistake."

Becky stared down at her baby. Jiggy was licking her toes, making her laugh hysterically. "He's repeating that with Logan." It was so sad, but what could they do?

"He's afraid Logan will end up like his mother. Wandering around, chasing dreams, but not happy. Indigo never grew up."

"You've met her." She must have.

"Oh yeah. That woman broke Logan's heart until the scars ran so deep I never thought he'd be able to love again." Her eyes burned with anger. "She'd show up for a day, talking about how her big break was just around the corner.

Then she'd take off again while Logan slept."

Becky couldn't stand it. "Doesn't she love him at all?"

"She does, but she loves herself more." Pricilla stared at the countertop. "I think the guilt made it hard for her to stay around Logan more than a day or two. He needed his mother, and she couldn't be what he needed. He was so lost for a while. It was heartbreaking and unnecessary. Indigo should have chosen her son over her career."

Becky began to get a sense of what they went through. "Why are you telling me this?"

Pricilla opened her mouth, but pounding on the door cut her off.

Jiggy scurried over, barking. Becky followed and opened the door. "Brian." Finally, one of them caved. Her father-in-law appeared to have aged as much as his wife. "Come in."

Pricilla stood by the couch, her eyes softening with hope. Even after all this, the woman loved her husband.

"I'll be in the bedroom. Come on, Jiggy." She wanted to give them privacy.

"Stay," Brian snapped. "This is about you."

Her? Butterflies jittered in her stomach as she paused by the table. "How so?"

Electric fury raged in his gaze as he stomped over and tossed down something on the table.

The air crackled as if a storm approached. The hair on the arms stood up. With her baby in her arms, she lowered her gaze.

"Recognize it? Your contract with my son for a temporary marriage. With a fifty thousand dollar payout."

No. It wasn't possible. "How did you get this?" No one was supposed to know. Becky couldn't look up, couldn't face them.

"It doesn't matter. You and Logan are in a sham marriage."

"Becky?" Pricilla picked up the pages and started reading.

She wanted to grab it out of her hands and rip it to shreds. To tell them it wasn't true. How had this happened?

"What's going on?" Pam's came into the room, rubbing her eyes. "Dad, you came."

Brian looked at his daughter then back to Becky. A tremor shook his hands and lined his voice. "You not only entered into a scam on me and the courts, but you deceived my wife and daughter. They love you. Pam looks up to you. And it's all a lie. A goddamned lie!"

Becky jumped at his rage. Sophie yelped, and started to cry. "No, it's not a lie. I love Logan."

"Don't you dare. It's all there in black and white. You're a gold-digging whore and I want you off my ranch today."

"I need to talk to Logan." She didn't know what to do.

"It's true?" Pricilla stopped flipping pages. "You married him for money?"

"No! I don't want the money. I married him to keep Sophie. I can't lose her. She's my baby." Tears burned her eyes and scorched her nose. "Logan is helping me."

"You're both liars. I'll deal with Logan when he gets home." He stepped closer. His eyes slid to Sophie. "You used your baby to get to us all. What kind of woman does that?"

"I…" Oh God. What could she say? "I didn't want to hurt you."

Pam lifted her gaze from the pages in her mother's hand. Her eyes shimmered with tears and betrayal. "You lied to us? Why? For money?"

"No. Pam, please, don't believe that."

"I trusted you. I've babysat Sophie, played with her, loved her. I wanted to be her Aunt Pam." She choked on a sob.

Pricilla hugged her daughter.

Brian put his hand on his wife's shoulder. "Go pack. I'm taking you home."

Pricilla closed her eyes, her shoulders sagging. Grooves dug into her face, adding ten years to her.

Becky had done this. She'd hurt two women who'd treated her and Sophie like family. Pricilla had been confiding in her this morning. All the things Becky had longed for all these years…

She'd had it. A family in all their dysfunctional glory. They had been hers. Until they learned of her deception. "I'm sorry." She barely got the words out. Sophie sensed her distress and buried her face in Becky's neck, sobbing.

Pricilla led Pam down the hall. They had nothing to say to Becky.

"If you get out of this house and out of my son's life today, and don't return, I won't give this to the social worker or courts. But if you so much as talk to Logan, or take one dime more of his money, I'll turn this over to them."

The full implications of his threat stabbed her chest. "You can't. I'll lose custody." Oh God. No. "She's just a baby. Please, Brian." She reached out to him in desperation. "Don't do it. Dylan doesn't want or love her."

He jerked back, evading her touch. "That's my only warning. Get out and stay away from Logan. From where I'm standing, the kid would probably be better off with the Ridgemonts than you. Don't test me."

Ice cold fear for Sophie seared her veins. "I'll go." She couldn't fight this. She headed for the room to pack.

Logan. What would he think when he got home and she was gone? She'd leave a note or something. At the bedroom door, she spun around. "I'm leaving, I'll do exactly as you want under one condition."

"Money?"

What else would anyone think who'd found that contract? Greasy nausea churned in her stomach. "No. Give Logan his land."

• • •

Turning into the Knight Ranch, Logan breathed a sigh of relief. He wanted nothing more than to get home to his wife and Sophie. He even missed Jiggy.

Once he'd thought he'd have to live alone, that it was the only way he could cope. But then Becky came into his life, and when the ghosts in his mind surged, her touch calmed them. It dawned on him that this was what real happiness felt like. What if Becky decided not to stay?

You have to ask her to stay. Tell her you love her.

He sucked in a breath. He'd planned to take her to the hotel for a romantic evening, just the two of them, and tell her. But he'd let work interfere.

No more excuses. If he didn't tell Becky, didn't give her a reason to stay, she'd leave.

Arriving at his land, he pulled in the driveway, surprised to find it empty. Becky's car was probably in the garage, but he'd gotten used to his stepmom and sister's cars there.

Maybe they'd gone home.

Then he, Becky, and Sophie could have the house to themselves again, and he could tell his wife he loved her. Beg her to stay and be his permanent life partner. He couldn't lose her now. Getting out, he grabbed his duffle bag and quickly checked his gun to make sure it was secure.

He looked over at the house. It all appeared...empty.

Shit. Instincts had kept him alive. Something was off.

Dylan?

Anxiety pooled in his guts, spreading black dread. What waited for him in that house? No shadows moved across the huge front window, no sign of life. Logan tried to shake it off. They were just out shopping, or up at his dad's house. Or maybe they had gone riding.

He had to go in the house. A war broke out in his body: His muscles tried to grow roots straight through the ground, while his training demanded he be loose and ready for action. Logan eased his gun out but kept the safety on. Approaching the house, every step echoed in his head: *Not dead. Everything's fine. They are not dead.*

When he reached the door, he didn't hear a thing. Not even Jiggy's toenails scrabbling across the floor.

Wrong.

The dread grew, spreading in his lungs.

Don't go in. Can't go through the doorway.

Ice coated his skin in the blazing sun as he unlocked the door and eased it open. Silence, broken only by the low hum of the refrigerator. His gaze pierced his living room, dining room, and kitchen. Empty. No blood, no sign of a struggle.

They were just out somewhere. Maybe they all went to lunch. But where was Jiggy?

Go inside, damn it.

Sharp awareness boxed the ugly dread trying to pull him into that black pit that had lived inside him ever since that hideous day in Afghanistan. Logan took a breath. He had a job to do—take care of his family. He stepped through the door and kept going.

Down the hall, he turned to Sophie's room and froze in absolute shock at the empty space. Everything was gone, the crib…everything.

What the fuck? Logan spun, went in his room and yanked open Becky's drawers in his dresser. Checked the closet. All her stuff was gone.

She'd left him. Becky and Sophie had left him. Even Jiggy was gone. Why?

Pure reflex had him clear the last bedroom and two bathrooms. Pricilla and Pam were gone, too. Everyone left.

He was alone.

• • •

Becky hugged Ava. "Thank you for helping me."

"I don't like leaving you here."

"I won't be here long. I have to meet with the real estate agent. Whatever the offer she has on the place, I'll probably take it. I need the money." She was barely functioning, but she had to keep going for her baby. Ava had helped her by borrowing a truck, helping move Sophie's furniture, and she had stayed with Becky as long as she could. Becky couldn't have gotten through the last day and a half without her.

"Call me after you talk to her and find somewhere to stay tonight."

Becky refused to cry anymore. What good would it do?

She was so broken, so afraid. She'd already lost Logan; she couldn't lose Sophie. But how would she fight now? She'd made such a mess she didn't know how to fix it.

"Becky—"

She shook her head, cutting off the sympathy. "Go, Ava. I'll call you once I talk to the real estate agent and lawyer." That was another problem—how much was left of the retainer Logan had paid the lawyer? She had to pull herself together and figure all this out. She needed to sell her mother's rings today.

Ave nodded in understanding. "Kiss my princess for me when she wakes up." She got in her car.

Becky watched her pull away. Jiggy sat on the steps behind her, his eyes sad and slightly accusing. "I tried to write him a note, but I…" No more crying. Her head ached, she couldn't eat, couldn't sleep.

She'd just closed the door when her cell rang. Snatching it up off the counter, the name on the screen screamed at her.

Logan. He must be home.

What should she do? Everything in her cried out to just hear his voice. Talk to him. Desperation drove her to tap *answer* on her phone. Putting it to her ear, she spilled out, "I can't talk to you."

"Becky, what the hell? Where are you? What's going on?"

She leaned against the wall and closed her eyes. He didn't know; Brian hadn't talked to him yet. "Your father found the contract." Her legs gave out and she slid to the floor as she told him what happened.

"Shit, when? How? Why didn't you call me?" His voice

sharpened with accusation. "You just left."

She squeezed her eyes shut. Hot tears spilled down her face, but she clung to the last of her self-control. "What else could I do?"

"Trust me. You could have trusted me!"

His rage shot through the phone and hit her so hard, she gasped. How many times had he told her to trust him?

"I did. I trusted you and look what that got me. My copy of the contract was missing. Who do you think stole it? Not your mom and Pam, they were too shocked, too horrified to learn how I had betrayed them." Their hurt faces made her cringe in agony all over again. Anger was easier than her sick regret. "Who do you think rifled through my things and stole my contract? Then ran to your daddy? It was Kendra, the woman you kept telling me to stop worrying about. The woman I didn't want in my house, but it wasn't really my house, was it?"

And Logan hadn't really been hers, either. She loved him so much, was willing to give up anything but Sophie for him. She'd told him she loved him. But he didn't love her.

"Damn it, Becky, you should have called me. I'll fix this, you just have to trust me."

"No." She had nothing left. No tears, no hope, just a heart so shattered, she didn't know how to keep functioning. It hurt to breathe. "As long as I don't talk to you, see you, or take your money, your father won't turn that contract over to the social workers, and he'll give you your land. You got what you wanted. Now I need to figure out a way to keep Sophie safe. Good-bye."

. . .

"Don't you dare hang up!" Anger boiled up from Logan's soul. Years and years of agony and loneliness, of knowing no matter what he did or how hard he tried, he never truly belonged. She hadn't even called him; she just left. "So it was a lie. A goddamned lie."

"What?"

He barely heard her over the tears in her voice. That pissed him off more. "You said you loved me." He'd believed her. Was trying so hard to be the man she could love. "But at the first sign of a real fight, you bail." He shot his gaze around their room, so empty without Becky's things, Sophie's toys, even Jiggy sprawled out on the floor, snoring.

They'd really left him. The hot anguish mixed with explosive anger. The walls of his house pressed in with unbearable pressure.

"What choice did I have? I had to go. For Sophie."

Christ, her broken words hurt him as badly as his own pain. "I wouldn't let my father hurt you or Sophie. Don't you understand that?" How could this have all gone so wrong?

She didn't believe in him. Desperate to escape the walls closing in, he stormed out of the front door, seeing nothing except the red mist of blind rage. "You didn't trust me. I was trying to love you, trying—" The words shot out with uncontrollable force. "But you didn't give me the chance, you just left. Didn't even wait to face me, but snuck off while I was gone." And wasn't that all just too fucking familiar. How many mornings as a kid did he wake up and his mother had left again?

"Why would I think you'd fight for me or Sophie? You wouldn't listen to me be about Kendra. She belonged in your family more than I did."

The truth of that slammed into him, draining some of the air from his throbbing betrayal and rage. She'd tried to tell him Kendra shouldn't be at their house, and he'd shut her down. He opened his mouth, but she cut him off.

"You wouldn't even tell your boss about me. You hid me from your Marine friends." Her breath hitched into painful gasps.

Logan's guts seized and his chest clamped hard. He'd done that. He'd hidden her from the men he loved like brothers, and Becky thought he was ashamed of her. "No, it wasn't like that." His throat closed up at her broken sobs. But he'd never been ashamed of her; he was ashamed of himself for luring her into a marriage contract. Becky had done it out of desperation for her child. He'd known that from the start. And if his Marine buddies or Sienna had found out? That shit would get ugly. They'd be all over his ass, calling him on his bullshit. Then they'd have done whatever it took to help her defeat Dylan.

Logan would have lost the only leverage he'd had to have Becky and get his land.

The sheer, raw ugliness of what he'd done rendered him mute. The lies he'd told himself fell away. He hadn't done anything to really help her fight against Dylan. He could have had Sienna running checks, digging, finding any ammunition to keep Becky from losing Sophie.

"I have to go."

Panic clawed at his throat. "Becky, please, give me another chance. I won't let my father—"

"I can't. It's too late. I won't risk Sophie." She hung up.

Logan closed his eyes, the weight of what he'd done nearly dropping him to his knees. He'd lost her, lost his wife, child, and dog. And for what? A piece of land.

God, he was no better than his father. Brian had engineered a way to control Logan through a contract for his land. Logan had engineered a way to use Becky and her deep love for her child to keep his land, and have her in his bed. Then he'd gotten trapped in his own game by falling for her. He'd said he was trying to love her?

He was a damned liar.

He loved her so deeply he couldn't bear it, but didn't have the guts to stand up for his woman.

Turning, he faced the doorway to his house. Dread built that familiar black anxiety, not from the PTSD but the realization that in this moment...

His house was just a house.

Becky, Sophie, and Jiggy were his home.

It's too late.

Her words bounced in his brain. Logan stood there, alone on his porch, surrounded by the land he'd once thought the most important thing in the world. He scanned the horizon, the day so bright and clear he could see the pond, and the camp he'd poured his passion into taking shape.

None of it mattered without his family. So what was he going to do? Be a quitter like his mother?

Or fight to win the love and trust of his wife?

Easy choice. Logan scrolled his contacts on his phone, and hit call. Once his lawyer answered, Logan said, "Brody, drop whatever you're doing. I have an emergency. Here's what I need..."

A few hours later, Logan and Brody strode into his father's office.

Brian Knight shoved back in his chair, put his elbows on the arms, and steepled his fingers. "You don't need your lawyer. As long as your *wife* stays out of your life, the land is yours."

If it had been anyone else but his father, he'd have decked the man for what he did to Becky. "You had Kendra spying on us." He should have listened to his wife.

"Kendra was suspicious when you didn't know Becky was allergic to bees. And she pointed out that Pam had gone home with a man she barely knew, then was attacked by the same guy after she started hanging around with that woman."

Rage spattered across his mind.

"Kendra thought you were going to come home and marry her, not some—"

"Bullshit. I told her straight up we weren't anything more than friends. I don't give a rat's ass about her except that she will never come near my wife again. And if I read one word about Becky in her e-zine, I'll tell the entire world what a conniving, two-faced bitch Kendra is." If Kendra were a man, she'd be picking her sorry ass up off the ground and searching for her teeth.

"You're not getting this. You won't go near that bimbo again if you want your land."

Logan turned to Brody. "Let's do this."

His lawyer set the pages in front of him. "You sure?"

Never more sure, but he didn't bother to answer. Instead, he took the pen and signed.

Brody shoved the papers in front of Brian. "Sign here,

here, initial here."

His father's eyes hit Logan. "Another contract? I don't think so."

Anger, and the sick knowledge of how terrified and alone Becky must feel, churned up black rage. It took iron control to keep from attacking. "This is the deed to my land, and all rights to everything on it except my truck, weapons, laptop, and clothes, which I'm taking. It's yours." Uncrossing his arms, he slapped his palms on the desk. "Listen up, old man, if you ever threaten my wife and child again, I will rip you apart. Becky and Sophie are mine and no one threatens them."

He spun to walk out and saw Pricilla and Pam white-faced in the doorway. "Not a word from either of you. Becky rescued Pam from a rapist and took both of you into our home, and you turned on her because she did something desperate to protect her baby. You got your feelings hurt, while she's out there in total terror with no money or help trying to figure out how to survive and keep her child out of the clutches of a man who beat Becky badly enough to put her in the hospital."

He strode out to find his wife. He had to convince Becky that he loved her and would always put her and their family first.

Chapter Seventeen

Becky's head throbbed, her throat so sore it hurt to breathe. Sophie screamed in her car seat. They were both as sick as dogs. It took all her strength to get her baby into the house. She felt her baby's head—fever. Her poor girl.

"Mommy will fix it." She got out the liquid Tylenol and double checked to make sure she gave her the correct dose.

Jiggy stuck close to Becky as she gave Sophie a bath and then tried to get her to nurse. Her little nose was stuffed up and she cried in frustration. Saline, suction, and a vaporizer finally soothed her and Sophie fell asleep. They were both so tired, Becky put her in bed with her. Jiggy curled up with them.

Becky rubbed his ears, a wave of love for her pet threatening to make her cry. Again. But she couldn't cry or her own nose would stuff up miserably. She'd accepted the offer on the trailer, talked to the lawyer, and sold her mom's rings at a pawn shop and returned to the lawyer's office to give that money to her.

She'd bought them time.

Just don't think about the rings. Or Logan. God, just don't think.

Her head was swimming with throbbing agony, her arms so heavy. "Make sure I wake up if Sophie cries."

Jiggy licked her hand.

Finally, Becky closed her eyes, willing herself to rest. Tomorrow she'd get them someplace safer. Tomorrow…

"Stop. Please." The barking stabbed her brain. So loud it ricocheted in her skull like a pinball machine. She couldn't bear it. Something tugged on her shirt.

Becky swam up through heavy fatigue. Something niggling at her brain. But she was so tired.

A sharp pain cut through her confusion. She forced her weighty eyelids up. "Jiggy?" She struggled to get her bearings. Her dog was shaking her shirt like a rag doll. He must have caught her skin when he'd bitten her shirt. "What?"

Sophie lay next to her and—a thick, sickeningly familiar scent seared Becky's nose and throat.

Smoke. Oh God. The trailer was on fire. Becky grabbed her baby, hit the ground, and tried to crawl while carrying Sophie. They had to get out.

• • •

"She'd better be there." Logan's frustration hit the nuclear zone as he swung the truck around and headed toward Becky's trailer. He'd gone there a few hours ago and it had been empty except for Jiggy. If the dog was there, Becky would be going back, but he hadn't been able to wait. He'd been running all over Dallas checking the places she might go—the offices of her doctors, lawyer, and realtor—he kept missing her.

"Don't growl at me because you lost your wife," Sienna's voice through his truck's Bluetooth jerked him back to their conversation. "The wife that not one of us knew about."

He'd had to confess everything to get Sienna to cooperate and track Becky's phone GPS. Once a Marine's administrative assistant didn't break laws and hack into secure sites unless she believed the cause was worthy. "I have to find her. She doesn't know that I want our marriage to be real."

"Ease up, cowboy. I'm looking right at her phone's GPS coordinates. She's at the trailer. You charmed her into that ridiculous contract, you can charm her into keeping you."

Could he? He ground his jaw. "I had leverage then. She'd do anything for her baby. She trusted me to keep them both safe from Dylan." And now she was alone, no protection. Anxiety gripped his shoulders and neck, pushing him to hurry. "While they were at the ranch, they were safe. A punk like Dylan isn't going to tangle with me."

"You think he'd go after her if he knew she was alone?"

"I don't know. I didn't do shit to find out." God, he was pissed at himself. He'd been so focused on his own goals, so sure that his money and name would help Becky get full custody, he hadn't done anything more to find out. "The only good news is he probably doesn't know she left the ranch."

"You sure he doesn't know? The Ridgemonts own Ridgemont Communications…their holdings include a huge cell phone division."

The hairs stood up on his neck. If Si could track the GPS

on Becky's phone, so could the Ridgemonts. "Goddammit." *Calm the hell down.* "Dylan's not going to do anything. He hasn't made a move since he found out she was married to me. And there's the custody case. If he tries anything, it'll backfire."

"Think he really wants his kid?"

"No, he wants revenge on Becky and to make Sophie go away." Becky had told him Dylan didn't want Sophie, and he'd threatened her and Sophie that first day he'd approached her in the parking lot. "I think his family wants her to clean up Dylan's mess. But the social worker is all over them, just like she is us. He can't take a chance."

"Come on, you're rich. When you don't want to do a job yourself, you—"

"Hire it out."

"Damn it, Logan, you should have called us in on this right from the start."

"I'm asking you for help now, Sienna. Get the guys on Dylan, rip his life apart, and find out if he's got anyone watching Becky. Get everything you can."

"You really do care about her."

He turned down her little street and slowed by her trailer. "More than anyone or any—oh fuck."

"What?"

"Smoke." He saw a glow through the front window. His pulse jacked. Heart pounded. His mind cleared to razor sharp. "Trailer's on fire, call it in."

Logan shot out of the truck and ran up the steps to the front door. Sounds of flames crackling warned him, but he felt the door. Hot. He wasn't getting in this way. Was that Jiggy barking? No time.

He ran around to the carport side of the trailer, cleared the steps, and pressed his palm to the door. Little warm. Tried the lock—open. He'd think about why that door was unlocked after he got his girls out.

As soon as he opened the door, he saw flames and smelled gasoline. Quickly, he assessed the flames roaring in the living room and heading for him in the kitchen doorway. *Go.* He raced in, hooked a right to the hall. The heat behind him was intense. "Becky!"

A bark. Right there in front of him. Logan dropped to his hands and knees and grabbed Jiggy's collar. "Show me."

The dog shot forward. Smoke rolled down the hall, filling every crevice. Flames crackled menacingly. They weren't going out the way he came in.

Didn't matter. He had to find them.

Jiggy led him straight, bypassing the baby's room into what had been Becky's mom's room.

A cough. They were in there.

Logan kicked the door closed, got to his feet and duck-walked to the noise in front of him. Using his cell phone light, he saw Becky at the waist high window, fighting to open it.

He angled the phone light to the floor. Sophie lay at her feet, barely crying. Logan shot to his full height and grabbed Becky by the arms. She flailed, trying to fight him in an adrenaline fueled panic. "Becky, it's me. Logan."

"The window won't open." Her voice was thin, broken. "Don't let Sophie burn. Not my baby, too."

Too. Like her family.

Her broken words ripped his heart out of his chest. He nudged her aside, and grabbed the window. Didn't budge.

Using his phone light, he saw the nail holding it shut. No time. "On the floor with Sophie. Hold the dog." He ripped the bedspread off and covered them. Then he wrapped his arm in his jacket and shattered the window. Shoved out all the pieces, and with another blanket he covered the remaining glass. "I'm handing you out first."

Flames licked beneath the door.

His heart pounded viciously. If that door went, and with the window open feeding the flames oxygen, they would burn. He scooped up Becky, got her out and on the ground.

Thank God.

He handed out Sophie and Jiggy. It was going to be a tight fit for him. Flames exploded through the door with a roar. Logan dove out the window, hit the ground, picked up his wife and daughter and got away as sirens cut through the night.

. . .

Becky didn't have her phone, wallet, money, or even her shoes. She sat on the hospital bed, holding her sleeping daughter.

She still didn't know how Logan had ended up at her trailer, saving them from the fire. Once they got out, all hell broke loose. Fire trucks and police cars screamed to a stop in front of the fully engulfed trailer. The paramedics got there soon after and wanted to take Sophie to the hospital as a precaution.

Logan stayed with Jiggy, swearing to take care of him.

The doctors determined Sophie and Becky had a virus and appeared okay otherwise after the fire. They treated both Becky and Sophie's viral symptoms, and now Sophie was asleep. All Becky had to do was figure out who to call to come get them, where to go, and how to survive.

Had her car made it through the fire? Even if it did, the keys were in her purse, which she assumed burned with everything else she owned. Besides, she couldn't sleep in a car with her sick baby. She had nothing, not even diapers for Sophie.

Every time she closed her eyes, she saw flames and tasted bile.

"Becky."

She jumped at his voice.

Logan stood at her bedside. His dark hair was shoved back, his clothes torn and bloody.

Bloody. "You're hurt." Her gaze shot back to his face. A cut slashed over his cheekbone, and his arms and hands had more injuries. She'd been sitting here thinking about herself and he'd been hurt.

"It's nothing." He laid his hand on Sophie's back. "Doctor said she's okay." He lifted his eyes to hers.

She loved his light green eyes, tried to drink them in. Imprint them forever. "I didn't wake up. Neither of us did. We were sick. Jiggy woke me." Where was her little guy? "Where is he?"

"He's at a house. Safe. He's fine, I promise."

Tears pooled in her eyes. "Don't take him from me. Please, I'll find a place that takes dogs." She wasn't being rational, knew in her heart Logan would never take her dog from her, but she couldn't help it. It was just too much. How ironic that she'd finally sold the trailer and it burned down. Freaking perfect.

"Don't cry, sweetheart. No one is taking Jiggy from you." He sat on the bed. "I meant that Jiggy is at the house we secured for you. He's waiting for you. He can't come in the hospital or I'd have brought him with me."

Relief sagged through her. "Somewhere for us to stay? Me and Sophie? I don't have my purse, or ID, or ATM card to get money out. I pawned my mom's rings, but I gave that money to the lawyer."

His jaw clenched. "I've been searching for you. I had Sienna track the GPS on your phone. You wouldn't answer my calls or texts. I had to find you."

"Why? Why would you risk it? Your dad is going to hear about this."

His eyes blazed. "I'd never let him hurt you, Becky. Ever. Brody drew up the paperwork, I signed over my land and the buildings to my dad. Camp Warrior Recovery is on hold."

His words ran together in her head, formed clumps, and spun. It didn't make sense. The whole reason he wanted the deal was to get the permanent deed to his land so he could build the camp. "Logan, no. Your land and camp is everything to you."

"Wrong." He stretched his legs out next to her and pulled her into his side. "You have no reason to believe this, but I know I screwed up. I'm your husband, the one person in the entire world you should know has your back. But you didn't know that because I didn't have the guts to tell you I love you. You really thought I'd choose the land over my girls?"

His girls?

"You love me?" As soon as the words were out, she was desperate to call them back. She was sick, had a fever, had been through a fire, and was probably hearing things out of pure desperation.

Rubbing his hand on her arm, he said, "I don't think I understood how much I love you until I came home and found you gone. You've had a horrible night and a rough few days. I don't expect you to forgive me right away, but I'm asking you to give me a chance to prove that I love you and can be worthy of you. I'm going to protect you until I know you and Sophie are safe. That part is not negotiable—the fire tonight wasn't an accident, it was purposely set in your living room."

Becky was still trying to take in that he was here and loved her. Wanted to prove himself when his last sentence sank in. "Someone was inside my trailer?"

"Yes." A nerve ticked in his jaw. "The windows were all nailed shut. They used an accelerant, probably gasoline."

The horror caused her to lean into him, seek his strength, his warmth. Memories of the fire that took her father and brother swirled with tonight's events. "I'm scared."

Logan put his arm around Becky's shoulders. "You're not alone. I'm staying with you. My friends from Once a Marine are on their way as we speak and already working on the case."

She tipped her head up, cold determination forming in her gut. "It's Dylan. He tried to kill his own child."

"He went after *my* wife and child. I'm going to destroy him. He'll never threaten you again."

"Yours? Even Sophie?"

He brushed her hair back, his mouth kicking up at the corners. "She had me the minute I held her in my arms on the horse."

Logan had come for them. It was starting to fully sink in. "You really gave up your land? For us?"

The fury in his eyes melted into warm pools. "I gave up my heart for you. It's yours. The land and my dreams are nothing without you to share them with."

Her heart swelled. She was sick, dirty, and homeless, but she had a real family.

• • •

Logan leaned against his truck parked outside the Lustor Nightclub. He had a score to settle.

"I can't figure it out." Hunter Reece shifted, his cold-eyed stare scanning the parking lot. "Where the hell does your pretty little wife put all that food she eats? Never seen a woman eat so many fajitas. I mean they were good, but damn."

Logan smiled despite the reason they were there. "Becky was starving today. She and Sophie are feeling better." Becky had lost a few pounds, but judging by the way she'd attacked dinner they'd cooked together for his friends, she'd get back up to fighting weight soon.

"She's a special woman, and that baby…man that kid's got some killer eyes on her. If she ends up with her mom's smile?" Hunt shoulder bumped him. "You're going to need my sniper skills when she's a teenager and starts dating."

"Oh hell no. Sophie's not dating." God. Just the thought… Nope.

A truck pulled into the parking lot, slid into a spot, and cut the engine. Dylan jumped out and swaggered toward the VIP entrance.

Time to focus on the job. Okay, technically this wasn't part of the job; this was pure revenge and staking out his territory.

Becky and Sophie belonged to him.

Logan shadowed the man across the parking lot to the back VIP entrance door. Just as Dylan reached for the door, Logan sprang, grabbing his wrist and spun him.

"What the hell?" Dylan froze as recognition cut off his outrage. "Knight."

"That's Mr. Knight to you, ass wipe."

Understanding filled his eyes. Backed in a corner, Dylan puffed up his chest. "You can't harass me like this."

"Okay, then how about like this?" Logan grabbed Dylan's shirt, lifted him off the ground, took three steps, and slammed him against a wall.

Shock dropped Dylan's mouth open.

Logan got serious. "I'd love to rip your fucking face off, so if I were you, I'd shut up and listen. You're done, Ridgemont. You're going back to prison and all your lawyers and family connections won't be worth piss."

Calculation chased out some of the fear in the bastard's eyes. "You're bluffing. They're going to clear my name. Prove that bitch was driving—"

Logan jerked him forward and slapped his head back up to the wall. "You're a real slow learner, Ridgemont. That bitch is my wife and I'll kill for her. Which, by the way, I'm trained to do."

Hunter leaned his shoulder against the wall, facing Dylan. "Logan is real messy about his killings, too. See, now me? I like the clean shot. It's what makes me an excellent sniper. But cowboy here? He gets all enraged and does really gross things with his knife…makes me want to puke." He sighed. "Sometimes I take the kill shot because that screaming just grates on my nerves."

Dylan swung his head back and forth. "You can't touch me. I'll file charges—"

"Do that when the police come to arrest you for attempted murder of Becky and Sophie."

He shook his head. "You've got nothing."

Logan leaned in so close, he could smell the expensive alcohol and rancid sweat. Silently he thanked his Once a Marine buddies—they'd found the goods on Dylan. "Garrett Lunger has been arrested. Turns out, he wants to save his own skin. He's told the cops and D.A. all about the man who hired him to kill Becky and Sophie." In a fire meant to terrify Becky in her last moments. Logan wanted to hurt this rat bastard in a bad way.

The color leeched from Dylan's boyish face. His hands on Logan's arms slipped off. Panting like a caged animal, he blurted out, "No. I don't know him. Cops can't connect me."

Sirens blared as cars pulled into the nightclub. Dylan struggled, trying to escape.

Logan's rage fought his self-control. The need to beat Dylan into a mass of pure agony, then lock him in a room and set it on fire pounded in his brain.

"Stand down, cowboy. You're just holding him for the cops."

Hunter's calm voice cut through the red haze demanding vengeance. For Sophie's sake, they had to do this legal or he'd jeopardize Becky getting full custody. The cops would overlook this little chat, but if he crossed any real lines…

Logan dropped his hands and stepped back.

The police swarmed in. A uniform spun Dylan, shoved his face against the wall, and cuffed him. "Dylan Ridgemont you are under arrest for…"

It was over. Logan walked away. It was time to go home.

• • •

"It's really over."

Logan eyed his wife hugging herself and gazing out the window into the dark night. "The nightmare with Dylan, yes. You'll get custody. Sophie will be safe."

She nodded, but said nothing else.

Logan had been patient for three days. Becky had been sick and when he wasn't taking care of her and Sophie, he'd been working the case with all his friends. He'd also made sure to notify the courts and social worker of their address change.

And every night, Becky slept in his arms.

But what would happen once the custody case was final in just two weeks? Would Becky fully forgive him for not putting her first when he should have? It'd be so much easier if he could keep supporting her, if she needed him to provide for her and her daughter. Then he'd have more time to get her to love him enough.

His mother had loved him, but not enough. Indigo could have stopped touring and lived nearby, gotten her life together and proved to the courts she could be a mother. She hadn't done that. It hadn't been until he'd seen what Becky would give up for Sophie that he'd finally realized the truth.

His mother was a flake. She'd kept Logan as long as he fit her life, but she wouldn't change for him.

Becky had given up her dream of being a nurse, or at

least put it on hold, and kept Sophie. She'd cared for her dying mother with a newborn. Becky stuck when she loved.

He wanted her love to be real, the kind that stuck no matter what happened—even when he screwed up. He had to give her the chance to choose, free of financial pressures and worries about her daughter.

Enough. Logan went to his dresser and got out the first item. Going to Becky he put his arms around her. "This is yours."

She tilted her head down.

He opened the small square box.

She gasped. "Logan. My mom's rings." Her hand trembled as she took out the two gold bands with the single diamond. She lifted her gaze. "I thought they were gone."

"I had Brody buy them back as soon as the pawn shop opened the next morning." He turned her, sliding the rings on her right hand. "You won't sell them again."

"Thank you." Tears spilled over her cheeks. "They are all I have left of all of them. Everything else is gone. But when I look at these, I remember not only my mom, but my dad and Tyler, too." She threw her arms around him. "Thank you so much."

He pulled her tight, wanting to bind her to him forever. "It's my pleasure, baby. You can give them to Sophie someday, and she'll have a piece of her grandmother."

She showed him her tear filled brown eyes. "You understand."

"I do." Framing her face with his palms he wiped her tears. Becky smiled and cried and rarely hid what she felt. He loved that, but he wanted to be the one to kiss her smiles and wipe her tears. "I have something else that's yours." He handed her a folder.

She frowned. "What is it?"

"Your savings account with fifty thousand in it. There's another smaller account for Sophie."

The blood drained from her face. "You're leaving?" She shook her head and shoved it back at him. "I don't want this. I don't want your money."

He tossed it to a chair. "Listen to me, I'm staying. I love you and Sophie. I will do everything in my power to keep you both. You're my family."

"Then why?"

"I want you to love me enough to stay, not because of what I can give you. You're both free, you have enough money, you don't have to stay." He wasn't sure if this was making sense, but he'd held back from her once, tried to protect his heart, and Becky had ended up alone and not knowing how he felt. Never again. So he told her the ugly truth. "No one's ever loved me enough to stay."

"I do and so does Sophie. You're her father." She closed her eyes, regret squeezing her face. "I only left because your father threatened Sophie. Otherwise, I'd have talked to you." When she opened her eyes, gold shimmered in her orbs. "I would have fought him for you, but Sophie is a baby. I have to protect her first."

"Damn right. Don't ever change that, Becky. It's one of the things I love about you. You didn't know what I'd do to keep you and Sophie safe. The difference is now we can protect her together. You won't ever have to wonder where I stand—I stand with you to protect our daughter."

Not long ago, those words—father and daughter—would have terrified him. Now they gave him his dream, the one he hadn't even wanted to admit to himself. "You're my family."

"We are." She burrowed into his arms, all her soft curves fitting against him. "I love you, Logan. I won't leave again."

The moment was perfect.

She looked up. "But you have another family. I invited Pricilla and Pam over tomorrow."

His face hardened. "No. And I don't want to talk about them. This is our time."

"That wasn't a question, cowboy. This is my home too and I want them here."

"You forgive them?"

She shrugged in that thin robe. "There's nothing to forgive. They thought I was using you for money. They love you, Logan. They barely knew me."

Oh, he wasn't letting them off that easy. "They lived in our house for over a week because you're so tender hearted. They knew you well enough."

"Forgive them, Logan. All they did wrong was defend you. Abby's coming, too."

He stared at her, his sweet girl with so many layers. "You're not going to budge on this, are you?" Becky had a spine of steel.

"I love you too much to let you throw away your family. And before you start ranting, your father isn't invited. I'm pissed as hell at him. He should never have let you sign your land over to him. That camp is important."

He couldn't help it, he smiled. "You're sexy when you defend and take care of me."

"You're mine. I take care of what's mine. Tomorrow is for family. Tonight..." She stepped back and let her robe slide off her shoulders, "is just for us."

Chapter Eighteen

"What do you think?" Pricilla wrung her hands, clearly anxious.

Becky looked around Spinners. On the wall over the mechanical bull was a huge sign, "Congratulations Logan, Becky, and Sophie!" Caterers had tri-tip, chicken, and sides spread along one wall, a three-layer cake dominated a corner. Guests milled around, dancing and celebrating.

Yesterday, they'd had the custody hearing for Sophie. Becky secured full custody, and Dylan had no visitation. The next step was going to be terminating his parental right so Logan could adopt Sophie.

"I know it's not fancy or—"

Becky turned to her mother-in-law and hugged her. "It's perfect. Thank you for doing this." She didn't want to know how much it cost to get Mac to agree to close Spinners on a

Saturday night.

Pricilla hugged and released Becky. "I wanted to, Becky. I love you and my granddaughter. Say you believe me. I still feel awful that we turned our back on you when you needed us the most."

"We've been over this, it was as much our fault. I should never have agreed to deceive you and the family. Logan and I were both wrong."

Pricilla nodded. "I wish I could fix this with Brian and Logan. Neither will make the first move. Brian's sitting home while we party." She shook her head. "He's going to end up a bitter old man."

Becky rubbed her arm. "You decided to stay with him."

"You probably think I'm a foolish woman."

"Far from it. You don't want to lose your family." The old pain stung. "I lost most of mine and would have given anything to have them back, faults and all. We'll heal this rift between Brian and Logan someday. In the meantime, he's Sophie's grandfather and he has the right to see her. Logan isn't fighting me on that."

Pricilla laughed. "Cause he'd lose. You're a heck of a lot fiercer than I gave you credit for."

"It's easy when I know Logan loves me just as I am."

"Thank you for understanding about Brian. I wanted him to love me the way Logan loves you, but I can't make him. But he did apologize to Pam. They've been spending more time together, and that makes me happy."

"You don't have to explain." She hurt for Pricilla. "He loves you, he just can't say it." Becky had seen how angry Brian was that Becky's deception hurt Pricilla.

Logan strode up with a few other people in tow. "Sophie

wants her grandmother." He handed the baby over.

Pricilla's eyes lit up. "Here's my darling girl. Let's go look at the cake."

"Good luck with that." He grinned at Sophie. "All she wants to do is sit on the mechanical bull."

"Such a tomboy. You're going to be just like your Aunt Abby, aren't you?" Pricilla's voice trailed away.

"Becky." Logan put his arm around her. "This is Adam Waters."

"Hi Adam." She held out her hand to the man with the tawny eyes and killer smile. "Thank you for all you and your security agency did to help us. Sophie—" She glanced over to see Pricilla holding Sophie on the unmoving mechanic bull. "She and Logan are my world. I'm beyond grateful."

"No need. We'd have been there from the start if we'd known." He released her hand and flashed a hard look at Logan before returning to her. "Don't ever hesitate to call any one of us if you or Sophie need something." Pulling a beautiful redhead into his side, his face softened. "This is my wife, Megan."

Forgetting the men, she grinned. "You're the veterinarian with the little boy. It's great to meet you." Becky dropped her gaze. "Looks like little Cole will be having a brother or sister soon."

"Great to meet you, Becky." She patted her baby bump. "Four more months. Next time we visit, we'll bring Cole so you can meet him. He's staying with my mom."

"So how do you juggle work and kids?" They wandered off to a table.

"It's going to be harder with a second one. I may take on another vet and cut back to part time. Adam and I are talking about it. But I couldn't do any of it without my mom." Megan glanced over to her husband. "Adam didn't know about Cole for the first couple years of his life. I was a single mom."

"I bet that's a story."

Megan laughed. "Oh yeah. I'll tell you sometime. But right now, why were you asking about balancing work and family?"

"I'm going back to school to finish my nursing degree. Or I think I am."

"Is that what you want?"

"Once it was. But now…I'm not sure."

Warm hands settled on her shoulders. "Sugar, you're going. Even if you never use your degree, it'll still be yours. Finish it."

Megan's light blue eyes moved up to Logan, then drifted down to her. "He's right. Love doesn't mean giving up your dreams. It means you work together to make both your dreams come true." She tilted her head toward the mechanical bull. Abby had somehow gotten Sophie from Pricilla and the two of them were sitting on the bull. "Looks to me like Sophie will be well cared for if you and Logan aren't home."

Her baby's shriek of delight sounded over the music and voices, and Becky's heart swelled. How could anyone have this much joy? She put her hand on Logan's. "That means your dream, too. Even if we have to start from the ground up, we're going to build Camp Warrior Recovery."

Adam pulled up a chair by his wife. "What can we do to help?"

Becky leaned forward. "We're going to need the perfect

location. We want a ranch environment, outdoors and away from civilization. These men and women need a chance to get away from the pressure of trying to assimilate back into civilian life while coping with their PTSD symptoms."

Becky flushed. "You were probably asking Logan, not me. He can explain it better." She wasn't the one who had dealt with combat PTSD and spent all the time and money working to build the camp to help other veterans.

Logan angled his head down to catch her eyes. "You explained it perfectly." He squeezed her shoulder. "You're so going back to school. We need you at Camp Warrior Recovery. Get your RN then you can specialize and help these vets."

"You mean that?"

Hunter dropped into the seat next to her. "Compassion and understanding like yours goes a long way, Becky."

"She volunteered at a VA hospital in high school and college. Becky's talked to a lot of veterans." Logan's eyes consumed her. "I didn't even realize how much she'd absorbed until just now."

The idea took hold of her. Excited her. "I'll call my guidance counselor, see what the options are. Oh, and maybe I can—

"Logan."

Pam's strained voice cut her off. Becky swung around in her chair to follow Pam's pointed finger. "I'll tell him to leave if you want."

Brian Knight stood just inside the door. His graze traveled the room.

Voices fell off as people realized who had come to the party.

"No." Becky jumped up and dug her fingers into Logan's arm. "Brian made the effort, he can stay if he wants."

Logan's mouth thinned.

Ava slipped up to Becky's side, holding Sophie. "He threatens you and I'm going to neuter him."

Becky briefly wondered when Ava got possession of Sophie. "He only did that when he thought I was using his son."

Ava glared. "He threatened my goddaughter, Becky. I don't forgive that."

"You will. He's her grandfather."

Brian's gaze landed on them and he made his way over. Whispers started, then built. By the time Brian stopped, they were surrounded by everyone there. All their family and friends including Lucinda, Mac, Brody, all Adam's buddies from Once a Marine.

Brian faced them both.

Logan shook off Becky's fingers and put his arm around her in a possessive gesture. "Becky won't let me throw you out."

She rolled her eyes. "Brian, you're welcome here. Dinner should be ready soon. Would you like a drink?"

Surprise softened the deep lines in his face. "I have something to say." He took a deep breath. "I'm proud of you both. Logan, you stood up like a man, defended your wife and child and chose them. And Becky, you did what you thought best to protect your child. After I'd made it clear you were to leave with nothing but the stuff you brought, you asked for one thing—that I give Logan his land."

Logan swung his eyes to her.

"I told you that. Besides, it didn't work. You signed it

away for me and Sophie."

He pulled her close. "I'd do it again. No regrets."

Brian regained their attention. "I regret that I ever let you go, son. I should have gone after your mother that very first day she left."

Logan turned. "Why didn't you?"

"My father stopped me. Told me to choose, either you and Indigo, or the ranch. I was so humiliated and felt so betrayed by Indigo, that I chose the ranch. Took me eight long years to grow the balls I should have had that day and go get you back. I was furious when I found out the life you were living. It was one thing for Indigo to betray me, but you were a kid. She had you sleeping in bars, or sometimes alone on the bus while she performed in dives." He shook his head. "When Kendra brought me that contract detailing your and Becky's temporary marriage, I felt betrayed all over again."

Becky fought a cringe. They had deceived him.

Brian went on. "Logan, in the end, you had more integrity than I did. You stood by your family, and now that I've had time to think, I respect that." He turned to Becky, handing her an envelope. "The deed to Logan's land. My son made a stand and I won't insult him by returning it. He wouldn't take it. He chose you, and he won't go back on that. So this is my wedding gift to you, 100 percent free and clear."

Becky ignored the envelope, slipped from Logan's hold, and hugged her father-in-law. "Thank you, Brian."

He seemed startled, his arms hanging at his side.

She leaned back. "I'm sorry, too. We tried to scam you, and we ended up hurting all of you."

His eyes softened and he hugged her. "Accepted. Can I hold my granddaughter?"

Becky took Sophie from Ava, and handed her to her grandfather. "You don't have to ask. We're family."

Brian smiled, his eyes lighting up when Sophie went right into his arms.

Pricilla put her hand on his arm. "I'm proud of you."

Brian shifted Sophie and curved his hand around Pricilla's hip. "I love you, Pris. More than any other woman. I'll say it every damned day, just don't leave me again."

She sucked in a breath. "I've already come back. You didn't have to say it."

He smiled her at. "I know."

Pricilla closed her eyes and leaned into her husband.

Logan turned Becky to face him. Taking her hands, he smiled. "You're wearing your mom's rings. She's here with us, too."

Her throat filled at that. For a fleeting second, she could almost feel her mom there, telling Becky that she loved her and wanted her to be happy, but that it was time for her to go be with Becky's father and brother. She and her mom had gone through a lot together, Becky could let her go with peace, knowing her father and brother would care for her now.

"She knows Sophie and I are happy, loved, and safe."

"And?" He reached behind him on the table.

She didn't know what he meant. "What else is there?"

He held up a small black box and lifted the lid. "You're mine."

Glittering beauty shimmered against black velvet. "Logan, it's breathtaking." A white gold engagement ring with three diamonds. Nestled next to it was a slender band encrusted with diamond chips.

He slipped the rings out, and put them on her finger. "You're my wife, my lover, and my friend. I want the world to know that I love you, cherish you, and I will stand by your side and guard your back all of our days together."

She threw herself at him, knowing he'd catch her and hold her. Always.

Acknowledgments

I'd like to thank Alethea Spiridon Hopson for working so hard to help shape this book, and for always being the calm in the storm! You make the impossible seem possible every single time. And a special thanks to Kate Fall for whipping the first draft into a stronger book.

To all my friends who listen to me whine whenever I hit a wall in writing a book, thank you for not changing your phone number or email address, or blocking me on Twitter and FB. You guys rock and keep me sane!

To my husband, because you believe each and every day.

About the Author

Jennifer Apodaca is the author of a mystery series and sexy romances. During the full moon, she releases her wicked side, named Jennifer Lyon, to write her dark and steamy paranormal novels. Her books have won several awards and been translated into multiple languages, but her greatest achievement is a happy and satisfied reader.

Jen lives in Southern California with her heroic husband, their three sons and Bailey, the sweet and spoiled dog. Jen loves to write, bake, read and hang out with her family. She sincerely believes that the four major food groups should be coffee, Diet Coke, chocolate and wine.